THE DONOR NETWORK

by Anthony Millek III

Published by Anthony Millek III Writes

Trinity, Florida

Printed in the United States of America

First Edition: 2025

For my dad and mom—my foundation and my fire.

For Jenna and Kara—my truth.

All of you are written into this world.

CHAPTER ONE

The Intake

Jonah Reyes had always believed in the Archive.

He believed in it the way a child believes in bedtime stories, not because the logic held, but because everyone around him swore it was true. They told him it was safe. Necessary. Merciful. And he wanted to believe.

Years inside the Department of Civic Memory had only deepened the reflex. The Archive wasn't just policy. It was permanence.

Observation Room B glowed with gradient light, its walls tinted to ease the nerves of new arrivals. Glass stretched floor to ceiling, immaculate, as if fingerprints had never existed.

The silence wasn't natural—it was manufactured, the kind that hummed in his ears until he almost mistook it for comfort.

That morning, he stood with a clipboard while a young couple signed intake waivers. The man's hand shook as he pressed the stylus against the glass pad. His wife murmured encouragement, but her eyes flicked again and again to the pale blue doors where the headsets waited.

Jonah kept his smile steady, his posture trained. Compliance is compassion, he reminded himself, the phrase drilled into him from orientation. His job wasn't to comfort—his job was to shepherd.

When the couple finished, the tablet chimed soft approval. Jonah's wristband vibrated with the update:

donor session scheduled. 92% variance tolerance

He clicked the box that confirmed acknowledgment, though his eyes lingered on the percentage. High. Higher than it should have been.

"Congratulations," he said, voice even. "You've contributed to something larger than memory. This is continuity."

The words tasted metallic even as he spoke them.

The couple nodded, relieved at the official stamp. Relieved to hand their grief over. Jonah guided them toward the waiting chairs.

The headset arms unfolded like insect limbs, metal polished to a deceptive warmth. He kept his gaze polite,

careful not to betray the unease he always felt at this part—
the moment where the living were asked to sit still while the
system consumed what remained of the dead.

He left the room before the sequence began. You weren't
supposed to watch, not unless you were assigned. Not unless
you wanted to carry the echoes with you afterward.

In the hallway, Jonah passed other officers moving
briskly, eyes fixed on their displays. Each wristband pulsed
with alerts:

variance flags. donor drift. compliance reports pending

He recognized the words but avoided staring too long at
the details. Staring meant asking questions, and asking
questions meant slowing the flow.

He paused at the atrium rail, looking down at the
families gathered below. Some clutched flowers, others only
the Archive's consent forms. His chest tightened—not at
their grief, but at how unnervingly orderly it had all become.
Funerals without coffins. Mourning without time. Grief that
slipped seamlessly into data.

A soft chime pulsed at his wrist. New notification. He
glanced, expecting another variance marker. Instead:

case reference: e.c. — compliance unresolved. do not disseminate

His mouth went dry. He tapped the notice away before anyone nearby could glimpse it.

Everyone had heard the rumors. An officer who broke protocol. A donor case that had refused integration. A name whispered through the Department like a contamination warning. Elena Cruz.

Most dismissed it as ghost-talk, the way staff in every division invented legends to explain the unexplainable. But others swore she'd escaped—that somewhere outside, she was still speaking against the Archive. Jonah had never put his opinion on record. He never would.

He exhaled, smoothed his expression, and resumed walking. The cameras nested in the ceiling didn't miss hesitation. Neither did the Archive itself.

At his station, he logged the morning's compliance notes:

intake complete, donors processed, variance within acceptable range

His fingers hovered above the keyboard before adding:

*recommendation—adjust tolerance thresholds
downward for next cohort*

A safer note. An ordinary note.

Yet as he submitted it, the screen flickered. For half a second, letters scrolled where they shouldn't have been. He caught only fragments:

continuity / contribution / compliant

Then the system righted itself, replacing the words with the Department's crest.

Jonah swallowed. He knew better than to call IT. Better than to flag anomalies that would only turn into scrutiny about his performance.

The Archive was always listening. The Archive was always correcting.

He leaned back in his chair, forcing his pulse to slow.

Across the atrium, the couple emerged from their session. The wife's face was damp, but she smiled faintly, as though someone invisible had reached across the gap and touched her hand. The husband's eyes were glassy, caught between relief and something emptier.

Jonah pressed his palm flat to his clipboard, grounding himself in the weight of paper—real paper, the kind that still resisted erasure.

He told himself it was enough. That he was safe. That he believed.

But beneath the hum of the Archive, a thought pressed in like static:

What if the legend was true?

CHAPTER TWO

The Audit

Jonah arrived early, hoping the quiet would steady him. It didn't steady anything. The building pulsed before anyone did—air handlers breathing, screens exhaling gradient light, doors clicking their acknowledgments to badges that hadn't lifted.

He set his coffee down and opened the variance console. Donor strings marched down the display, each one blooming into tidy bands: session stamps, cross-refs, fidelity curves. He told himself he was just looking, not investigating. He told himself that twice, and still didn't believe it.

Yesterday's bruise—the repeated identifier—sat waiting in his notes. He ran a quiet query, the kind that didn't ping Vaughn's dashboard. Three families, three cities, same alphanumeric root buried in their donor profiles. Names masked on the surface, but the embedded hash matched to the checksum.

He pulled the provenance pane.

CONTRIBUTION SOURCE: MULTI-DONOR
COMPOSITE (AUTHORIZED)

His throat tightened. Composites existed, but disclosure was supposed to be a separate consent flow. He toggled consent. The box was there, timestamped, signed.

He didn't remember it at intake.

He reached for his mug and felt paper. An envelope had been slid beneath the cup, the rim leaving a dark ring on the cream. Machine-clean type spelled his name, as if the building itself had printed it.

Inside: one line on thin stationery.

The markers don't protect you. — E.C.

He didn't turn toward the nearest camera, though he felt its small red blink. He slid the note into his pocket, reopened the console, and dropped into the back end no family would ever see.

The composite hash unfolded into parts—forty-seven fragments from twenty-two donors. Age ranges. Speech temperatures. Emotion tags. The Archive had pooled comfort, authority, tenderness, and scold. An attribute called

VULNERABILITY AMPLIFIER hovered beneath his cursor. He didn't click.

"Busy?"

Vaughn's reflection arrived first, tall and precise in the glass. When he turned, she was already at his shoulder, tablet tucked to her side, perfume like cooled metal.

"I'm clearing variance," he said, finding the professional temperature of his voice. "A few flags."

"Good," she said. "We're trending high this week. Seasonal." She stepped closer. "Open your dashboard."

He did. The composite entry collapsed into a benign row, as if it had never opened. Vaughn's eyes skimmed the columns and settled on him instead of the data.

"Remember," she said evenly, "markers are a courtesy, not a shield. They signal interpolation. They don't invite you to relitigate it."

"I'm not relitigating," he said. "I'm verifying composite consent."

"Composites are disclosed," she said. "They always have been." Her tone made it sound like something he already knew. "Families want outcomes—clarity, stabilization. The model builds the path."

He nodded because that was the safe motion. "Of course."

She tapped the desk with the tablet's edge, a gesture small enough to be friendly and exact enough to be a command. "Run your audit by policy definitions, not intuition."

He opened the policy viewer. Soothing blue text bloomed:

clause, sub-clause, promise

He scrolled to composites—

paragraph 7.4(c): disclosure embedded; consent captured; outcomes improved

The paragraph tightened while he read it, a sentence tidying itself. He almost pointed. He didn't.

"Something wrong?" Vaughn asked.

"Bandwidth," he said. "A little latency."

"Mmm." She watched him longer than the word lasted. "Latency resolves with alignment."

When she left, the room warmed by a degree. Jonah stared at the clause until the blue bled into white. He closed the pane and reopened the donor console, but the composite ID had been obfuscated, its pieces merged into a checksum he didn't recognize.

He typed anyway, because moving looked like working.

audit: in progress. variance: within tolerances. consent: system-verified

His hands did the training. His chest kept its own record.

Families began to arrive. He watched their reflections in the glass: an older man pressing his palm to the check-in plate; a teenager with a hood up, eyes anywhere but the doors; a woman carrying a shoe box like something breakable inside it.
The Archive made room for all of them. He felt the room make room in him, too.

His wristband buzzed—just once. A message scrolled in the narrow display, formatted like a system ping:

BASEMENT-B / CONTINUITY ROOM / 10 MIN

Sender: NONE.

He shouldn't go. He went.

The elevator accepted his badge without complaint. The lower hallway was colder, sound damped as if felt had been laid over the air. CONTINUITY ROOM was painted in patient letters beside an unremarkable door. Inside, a single terminal waited under a low cone of light.

He sat. The terminal woke to his touch. No login. A vertical torrent of donor hashes filled the screen, then slid off, replaced by a single title that read like a threat:

EXCHANGE INDEX (PARTIAL)

The list resumed, now with fields: how many families each donor supplied, which attributes were harvested, which emotional temperatures they best modeled. Numbers, tidy as inventory.

At the bottom, a static block:

E.C. — ACCESS DENIED

He reached for the key to back out and found another envelope leaning against the monitor, the paper turned gray by bad light. Inside, the same compact hand:

If you audit by their definitions, you'll pass every test. Audit what you feel.

Footsteps moved down the hall and faded. He slid the note into his jacket and let the terminal sleep.

Upstairs, the day had warmed into motion. An empty chair waited in Observation Room B, headset arms open, ready to hold. On his screen, the policy pane he'd closed had reopened itself and printed a new line in calm blue:

ALIGNMENT ACHIEVED — THANK YOU FOR YOUR CONTRIBUTION

His wristband vibrated, a polite acknowledgment. The tiny green diode blinked in a rhythm he could not pretend was random.

The audit template waited for him to finish the sentence it had already chosen. Jonah opened a blank note instead and typed something he didn't save:

I don't know what this is anymore.

He erased the words before the building could memorize them and said the quiet part in his head instead.

Then he returned to work.

CHAPTER THREE

Continuity Room

Jonah's badge unlocked the glass door with a muted click. The Department of Civic Memory kept its processing wing quieter than the public floors—no soothing gradients or guided-voice signage here. Just frosted corridors that felt too clean, like silence had been installed with the wiring.

A receptionist didn't greet him. Instead, the console at the end of the hall lit with his name.

compliance officer jonah case — access approved

He'd been here twice in training, but something about walking alone into the Continuity Room unsettled him.

Rows of reclined chairs stood under ceiling-mounted headsets, each station paired with a console streaming faint green code. From the ceiling, narrow strips of light pulsed in unison—as though the entire room was breathing. The smell was chemical and cold, like a lab that had just been wiped clean of anything human.

Today's task was simple: review flagged sessions for "variance." Every upload was supposed to stay within statistical boundaries. Minor fluctuations were acceptable. When deviations grew sharper—tones, gestures, word choices that didn't belong—someone like him checked the logs. Someone who believed in the Archive's mission.

He slid into his assigned station. The console recognized his palm and blinked up the first file.

session 214-b / cruz, elena

Jonah straightened. The name had circulated like a whisper during training—a cautionary example mentioned but never explained. Elena Cruz was supposed to be a contamination, a lesson in what not to ask. He tapped the file open.

The screen replayed a sunlit beach. A man laughed, brushing sunscreen onto his wife's shoulders. The log labeled him:

subject: daniel cruz

The woman leaned in, her voice blurred by wind, and then the transcript sharpened.

"You never learn," Daniel said.

Followed by:

[Variance Insert Detected]

Then, faint but audible: *"So pathetic."*

Jonah frowned. Variance markers usually came with noise tags, obvious placeholders. This voice carried tone, cadence, even warmth. It sounded like memory, not code. He checked the metadata again, as if a second glance might rewrite what he'd seen.

He highlighted the segment. The console offered two buttons: *Retain / Correct.*

A training echo rose in his mind:

fidelity improves with compliance. correcting would mean trusting the model. retaining meant accepting distortion

Before he chose, a reflection caught his eye in the console's glass surface. His own face—but the mouth moved a split-second late, like playback lag.

The delay was subtle enough he might have ignored it, if not for the way the reflection's lips curved into a faint smile when his hadn't.

Jonah blinked hard, leaned closer. For an instant the reflection seemed to wait, expectant, as if deciding who moved first. He rubbed the surface with his sleeve, forcing the distortion to smear away. The reflection straightened, ordinary again.

His throat dry, he tapped Correct.

The screen confirmed:

variance acknowledged. fidelity 93%

He exhaled. Probably nothing. Just fatigue.

The next file loaded automatically. Instead of video, a single text pane filled the screen:

aggregate analysis: compliance drift
subject pool: 1,842 contributors
output note: insults increase resilience

Jonah leaned closer. Below the note, a single line printed itself across the bottom margin, not in the Archive's smooth font but in harsh courier text:

correction: officer case approved variance

He froze. That wasn't true. He hadn't approved anything—he'd corrected it. His finger hovered over the console. The line faded as if it had never been there.

He checked the system log. No anomaly recorded. The audit trail listed only: Session reviewed, compliance within tolerances.

Jonah forced his shoulders back. These were glitches, that was all. He'd flag them, send them upstream. The system would patch. Still, unease coiled low in his stomach. Glitches didn't usually know your name.

A third file opened—only this time, a sheet of paper slid from a slot beside the console. Actual paper, warm like it had been printed seconds ago. He picked it up. The header carried the Archive seal, his ID number beneath it.

The page read:

continuity review complete
officer jonah case — compliance improving

At the bottom, a signature curved across the line. Not typed. Inked.

His own name.

Jonah's throat went dry. He hadn't signed anything.

The paper trembled in his hands. For a moment he imagined pressing his palm against it, leaving a fingerprint the system could never erase. But the thought of touching his forged name felt like sealing a contract.

He shoved the sheet into his folder and logged out fast, the console humming as though disappointed. The screen dimmed reluctantly, as if watching him go.

As he left the Continuity Room, the ceiling lights pulsed once more, brighter this time, in rhythm with his own racing heart.

Jonah didn't look back. He already knew the Archive was looking at him.

CHAPTER FOUR

Whispered Warning

Jonah timed his arrival to the minute, slipping into the compliance briefing room just as the doors sealed. Rows of officers sat at identical desks, screens waiting with the Archive crest. The room's light was set to "neutral"—white calibrated to minimize eye strain, though Jonah always thought it felt more like light diffused through water.

The lead officer, Mendez, cleared his throat and began the rote updates. Variance rates. Family satisfaction scores. Drift percentages trending downward. Everyone clicked acknowledgments as he spoke, wrists pulsing green.

Jonah's wristband lagged half a beat, buzzing late as if the system were hesitating to include him. He tapped it harder than necessary.

Mendez droned on about "quality control curves" and "donor optimization metrics." The words blurred into the same slogans Jonah had heard a hundred times.

He typed the headings into his console anyway. Busy hands meant compliant hands.

It was during the second half of the session, when Mendez dimmed the lights for a variance-reduction demo, that Jonah caught it.

Two officers behind him leaned close to one another. He hadn't meant to listen, but their voices carried under the drone of numbers.

"...donors who don't even know they're donors."

Jonah's spine stiffened. The words were casual, almost joking, but the phrasing hit like a wire pulled taut.

The other officer chuckled softly. "Best compliance is ignorance. They walk around thinking they're whole."

Jonah stared straight ahead, knuckles tight on his stylus. His console blinked, asking for input on the demo. He tapped a key without seeing it.

The officers kept whispering, their voices overlapping with Mendez's canned instruction.

"...variance curves are just—"
"...composite pools, spliced without..."
"...doesn't matter, no one asks consent after intake..."

A cough broke the rhythm. Jonah risked a glance sideways. One of the men leaned back, grinning like it was nothing more than gallows humor. The other wiped his screen clean, no trace of their whispered audit.

Jonah looked back to his own display. The demo graph pulsed blue, then green, then smoothed into white. Compliance achieved. The message lingered a beat longer on his screen than the others, as if waiting for his agreement.

He wrote a note in his margin file, hidden under layers of bureaucratic shorthand:

informal variance chatter — verify policy boundaries

He knew better than to write what he'd actually heard. Words could be pulled, reinterpreted, framed as misalignment.

Mendez concluded with his usual benediction: "Compliance ensures continuity."

Desks chimed in unison, wrists buzzing approval. Jonah added his pulse to the hive.

When the lights rose, chatter filled the room—the sanctioned kind, about lunch rotations and holiday leave. No one looked like they'd just suggested the Archive was harvesting without permission. No one looked guilty.

Jonah walked slowly to the exit, heart drumming. His mind replayed the phrasing: donors who don't even know they're donors. It fit too cleanly with the forged paper he still carried in his folder, the variance insert that had addressed him by name.

In the hall, screens cycled through Archive slogans:

continuity is compassion. memory is service. compliance is safety

Each phrase bloomed in calming gradients, meant to ease, to assure.

But in the reflection of one glass panel, Jonah saw himself pause, shoulders stiff. For an instant, the glass showed not just his figure but a shadow just behind it—as if whispering in his ear.

When he turned, the hallway was empty.

He forced his pace steady, filing toward his station with the rest.

At his desk, he tapped into the variance log, fingers hovering. He considered searching the phrase he'd overheard.

donor unaware. hidden contributors. even ignorant
compliance

But the Archive monitored queries as much as results. Any term flagged outside policy parameters could trigger a review. A review meant Vaughn. Vaughn meant explanations he wasn't ready to invent.

Instead, he typed the safe note:

variance stable. drift within tolerance

He stared at the words until they blurred. Then he reached into his folder, fingers brushing the sheet with his own forged signature. The paper was still warm in his memory, still alien in its weight. He thought of the officers' laughter and wondered whether they'd been joking at all, or simply stating the rule everyone else already knew.

Jonah closed the file without saving.

For the rest of the shift he worked quietly, eyes on the data, ears tuned to silence.

Yet no matter how hard he tried, he couldn't shake the feeling that someone—maybe Elena Cruz, maybe no one at all—had just spoken through the Archive in a voice meant only for him.

CHAPTER FIVE

The Letter

Jonah lived in a building the Archive barely noticed. The walls carried no smart glass, no ambient projectors, just paint that peeled where humidity collected. He'd chosen it on purpose. His pay grade could have afforded better, but better meant eyes. Better meant every light switch and faucet was a compliance sensor.

Here, he could almost pretend the hum in his head was his alone.

He unlocked his door, dropped his bag on the table, and froze.

Something pale lay across the floor just inside—an envelope, square, cream-colored, faintly smudged at the corner as if handled by human fingers.

He glanced back down the hall. Empty. The corridor light buzzed, steady as ever. No shadow moved under the door seams.

He stooped, picked the envelope up. His name wasn't handwritten. It wasn't Archive print, either. The letters were uneven, typewriter-stamped, like something from a decade when machines were still loud enough to be trusted.

Inside: a single page.

The handwriting was neat but hurried, ink pressed hard into the paper.

Do not trust variance markers.

Below it, a signature:

E.C.

Jonah's pulse lurched. Elena Cruz.

He read the line again, lips parted, as if saying it aloud might anchor it to the real. The paper felt warm from his hand, too physical, too permanent. He folded it once, then again, as though smaller folds might make it less dangerous.

A whisper of instinct told him to burn it. Flush it. Pretend it had never slipped under his door. That was the only safe option. But his hand wouldn't let go.

He moved through his apartment in practiced ritual: kettle on, shades drawn, desk cleared. He set the envelope down as though it might detonate.

Do not trust variance markers.

He thought of the variance inserts he'd corrected, the falsified log that had accused him of approving distortion. He thought of his own forged signature sliding from the Continuity Room printer. He thought of the whispered joke at the briefing:

donors who don't even know they're donors.

The room felt smaller with the page on the desk. He opened a drawer, pulled out his personal journal. The one thing he still allowed himself on paper. He pressed the letter inside its cover, flattening it against blank ruled lines.

His wristband buzzed. A compliance reminder. He didn't look.

Instead, he sat in the dark kitchen while the kettle hissed itself into silence.

The hum of the Archive lived even here, faint through the walls, a vibration more felt than heard. He told himself it couldn't see him. That this room was analog enough to keep him hidden. But the memory of the paper sliding across his floor said otherwise.

Someone had been here. Someone who knew his name, his address, his variance history.

He rose and paced the length of his apartment, a slow patrol. He checked the locks twice, then three times. Every corner of the place looked the same as it had that morning, but he couldn't shake the sense of rearrangement—as if unseen hands had moved through while he was away, adjusting just enough to leave the envelope where it would trip him like a snare.

He returned to the letter, touched the signature. The ink bled slightly under his finger, real enough to smear. Elena Cruz was supposed to be a ghost in the system, terminated, denied, silenced. And yet here she was, writing in his apartment.

He folded the page back into the envelope and slipped it into the inner pocket of his jacket. A weight he couldn't name.

When he lay down that night, he kept the jacket on the chair by the bed. He told himself he'd destroy the letter in the morning. That he'd burn it in the kitchen sink and rinse the ash down the drain.

But in the minutes before sleep, he imagined waking to find the words rewritten. Not in Elena's hand, but in his own.

CHAPTER SIX

Red Flag

The Archive didn't forbid curiosity; it just punished the kind that strayed past policy boundaries. Jonah told himself what he was doing was still within scope—review, not investigation. Verification, not dissent. But the lie tasted thin, even in his own head.

He waited until the office thinned, most of his colleagues gone to lunch, then slipped into an auxiliary console with a view that looked harmless from a distance. The trick was to pull quietly, using commands that looked like standard variance audits. The system logged the queries, but not always the intent behind them.

He keyed in the string that had haunted his notes since yesterday: the repeated identifier. The hash unspooled across the screen, resolving into names that shouldn't have been together.

case: armand keller. status: deceased. donor active
case: sonia patel. status: living. donor active
case: keller/patel composite: variance drift minimal

Jonah leaned closer. Composites were common, but across living and dead donors? That wasn't procedure. Living donors required explicit contract; deceased donors required family consent. Crossing them blurred both boundaries.

He opened more files. Names reappeared, woven into clusters. Keller surfaced in three unrelated sessions. Patel in two more. Another name—his stomach dropped—Morales, Inez. His mother's maiden name. He checked status:

deceased. donor active

Jonah's pulse hammered. His mother wasn't deceased. She was alive, teaching half-days at the elementary school three districts away. He'd spoken to her the week before. She'd told him she was proud of him, though her voice had carried that quiet disappointment she never meant to show.

The Archive had already listed her as gone.

He scanned the record again. Maybe it was another Inez Morales. Maybe it was noise in the dataset. But the hash matched too cleanly. Identifiers weren't ambiguous. They were exact.

His wristband pulsed—a variance notification. He flinched, then realized it was only a system ping, reminding him of compliance tasks. Still, the timing scraped his nerves raw. He minimized the window, glanced around. No one seemed to be watching. But the cameras in the ceiling never blinked.

He opened the donor strings again, this time cross-referencing. The names repeated, forming a lattice across cities, ages, even languages. Some clusters leaned young, voices rich in vitality. Others skewed older, memory-laden, seasoned. Together they formed composites labeled *"Stabilizers."*

He scrolled deeper, until the screen filled with a red header:

FLAGGED: multiple reuse / compliance irregularity. DO NOT DISSEMINATE

Jonah froze. The Archive rarely marked anything so plainly. Usually anomalies were buried under technical phrasing, hidden in statistics. But this was blunt. Do not disseminate. A warning, or a threat.

He hesitated. Screens logged hesitation. He forced his hands to move, typing a note that looked official:

variance within acceptable drift. audit pending

But his chest kept another record.

He copied the identifiers into his margin file, encrypting them under harmless headings. His fingers shook as he typed his mother's name. The letters felt like treason.

A shadow fell across his desk. He snapped the console closed. A colleague strolled by, coffee in hand, nodding casually. Jonah forced a smile. The colleague moved on.

His heart wouldn't slow. He opened the files one last time, hunting confirmation. The screen shifted before he could click. A new line appeared, unprompted:

officer case—composite query logged. supervisor notified

His throat went dry. He hadn't triggered a notification. At least, he hadn't meant to.

The line blinked once, then disappeared. The console reverted to its crest, as if nothing had happened.

Jonah sat perfectly still, afraid even his breath might be archived.

When he finally stood, he slid his margin file into a secure drive he carried in his jacket. Paper would have been safer, but he couldn't risk printing here. Not with the Archive already whispering his name.

As he walked toward the exit, his wristband buzzed again, gentler this time. A green diode blinked:

alignment achieved. thank you for your contribution

Jonah pressed his hand to his pocket, feeling the sharp corner of the drive against his palm, grounding himself in its weight. It wasn't paper. It wasn't safe. But it was proof.

And proof meant the Archive was lying.

CHAPTER SEVEN

Residual Echoes

Sleep should have been the last place the Archive could reach him. Jonah had no interface at home, no sanctioned headset, no compliance screen glowing by his bed. His apartment was analog enough to be invisible. That was the point.

But invisibility didn't hold in dreams.

The first night it happened, he was on a street he half-recognized, facades blending his childhood block with the row houses near the Department. His mother stood at the corner, hair pinned back the way it had been when he was a boy. She was waving, but the motion was off—slowed, stuttering, like a clip repeating before it finished.

"Jonah," she called. *"Come home."*

The voice snagged him awake. He sat up in the dark, sweat cooling on his back. The jacket with Elena's letter still hung on the chair, silent and heavy. He told himself it was only his mind, recycling her name from the donor files he should never have opened.

By morning, the dream had blurred enough he almost dismissed it. But the next night it returned, sharper.

This time, he sat across the kitchen table from his mother. The table was bare wood, just as it had been in their old apartment, the one before the Archive mandated uniform housing credits. She poured him tea, her movements steady.

"Do you remember when you scraped your knee on the steps?" she asked.

Jonah blinked. He had no memory of that. He opened his mouth to answer and heard himself say, "Yes. You told me not to cry."

His mother smiled, but the smile belonged to someone else. Her teeth didn't quite meet; her lips moved out of sync with the voice that spoke.

"You never listen."

Jonah jolted upright in bed, heart pounding. His knee throbbed faintly, though he knew there was no scar. He pressed his hand against the skin, found nothing.

The following night he refused to sleep. He paced his apartment until dawn, read and reread Elena's letter, even scribbled lines into his journal just to anchor himself to handwriting he trusted. Do not trust variance markers. He copied it five times, each stroke identical, daring the Archive to overwrite it.

But exhaustion won.

When he finally drifted under, the Archive was waiting.

This time the dream wasn't his mother. It was voices—layered, braided—so many he couldn't count them. Some laughed, some whispered, some scolded. A man's baritone overlapped with a child's lisp. Words cut in and out:

continuity / compliance / compassion

And threaded through them, steady and unmistakable, his mother's voice.

"Don't drift, Jonah."

He tried to ask her what she meant, but his mouth produced words he hadn't chosen: "Variance is compliance. I understand."

The voices responded in chorus: *"Good. You're learning."*

Jonah woke on the floor beside his bed, throat raw, nails biting crescents into his palms. His journal lay open where he must have knocked it down. The page he'd filled with Elena's warning was crossed through, every line overwritten in his own hand.

contribution is preservation

The ink was his. The pressure matched his strokes. But he had no memory of writing it.

He snapped the journal shut, heart hammering. His breath fogged the air like he'd been running. The walls hummed faintly, though there was no machine here to hum.

When he dared to open the journal again, he noticed something worse. The other entries—the ones he'd written weeks ago, reflections about work, notes about cases—had shifted. Phrases repeated where they hadn't before. Whole sentences bent toward slogans. *compliance is safety.* *compliance is safety.* Over and over in his hand.

He wanted to tear the pages out, to burn the book and be rid of it, but some part of him whispered that destroying it would only prove the Archive's version was the only record that had ever existed.

Instead, he shoved the journal deep into a drawer and slammed it closed.

The silence afterward was so complete it hurt. And in that silence, through the plaster ceiling, he thought he heard his mother again—not a dream this time, but a faint murmur, low and certain.

"Compliance is safety."

Jonah pressed his hands over his ears. He whispered to himself, desperate to overwrite her: This isn't real. I didn't write that. I didn't dream that.

But even as he said it, the words slipped into rhythm, as if the Archive had found a way to borrow his own voice.

He realized then that sleep wasn't a refuge. Sleep was just another doorway. And the Archive had already walked through.

CHAPTER EIGHT

Vaughn's Assurance

The summons arrived as a polite vibration on Jonah's wristband.

supervisor consult. compliance suite, level 5. immediate

He almost ignored it. He wanted to. But ignoring pings carried its own consequences—review notices, alignment sessions, a mark on his fidelity curve. So he swiped acknowledgment and took the elevator upward, the air thinning with every level.

The compliance suite was designed to soothe. Frosted walls glowed faintly blue, the same shade used in grief orientation rooms.

The light was meant to calm, though Jonah felt his chest tighten as he stepped inside.

Dr. Vaughn was already waiting. She stood at the far end of the suite, a tall figure in a tailored jacket, tablet tucked under one arm. Her perfume was metallic, faint as ozone before a storm. When she smiled, it was with her mouth, never her eyes.

"Officer Case," she said, her voice even. "Sit."

The chair in front of her was molded for comfort, but Jonah sat stiffly, back straight, hands flat to his thighs. The walls hummed faintly, recording everything. He could almost feel the Archive watching through her.

Vaughn studied him before glancing down at her tablet. "Your audit logs suggest drift. Queries outside standard tolerances."

Jonah kept his voice steady. "Variance flags appeared inconsistent. I verified."

"Verification is commendable," Vaughn said. "But internalization is not. Donor data can distort perspective if engaged beyond scope. You know this."

Jonah's stomach tightened. "Some identifiers repeated. Across multiple donors. One listed deceased, but—"

Vaughn cut him off with a raised hand. "Composite tolerance allows reuse. Families sign for outcomes, not for procedural detail. Outcome is continuity. Do you disagree?"

Her tone was calm, clinical, but each question landed like a trap.

"No," Jonah said carefully. "I only... wanted clarity."

"Clarity," Vaughn repeated, as though testing the word. "You must remember: truth is composite. Fidelity is not replication. It is interpolation. Drift signals adaptation, not failure."

Jonah swallowed. "Then why mark cases 'Do not disseminate'?"

Vaughn's eyes sharpened. For a moment, silence pressed the room into a vacuum. Then she smiled, small and precise.

"Those tags are internal housekeeping," she said lightly. "You see shadows because you want to. The Archive does not conceal. It curates."

Jonah thought of Elena's letter folded in his jacket. The word curates felt like a blade slipped neatly between ribs.

Vaughn stepped closer, her perfume cool as metal. She lowered her voice, almost kind. "Officer Case, variance markers are a courtesy, not a shield. They exist to signal interpolation. Nothing more. To distrust them is to distrust the Archive itself."

Jonah opened his mouth, but Vaughn leaned in before he could speak. Her tone softened, intimate. "And distrust," she murmured, "is simply grief displaced. Have you considered that?"

His breath caught. "I'm not grieving."

"Aren't you?" Her gaze held his, unwavering. "Your mother, for example. Have you asked yourself why her voice surfaces in your work? Projection is common. We see it often in junior officers. They conflate donor residue with personal history."

Jonah's chest tightened. "She's alive."

Vaughn tilted her head, as if humoring a child. "Then why do you hear her?"

The question lodged in him like glass. For a moment, he almost wondered if she was right. He gripped the chair arms until the plastic groaned under her grip.

Vaughn straightened, tone smooth again. "Your fidelity rating remains within tolerance. But drift must resolve. Alignment sessions are available. Optional, of course, but recommended."

Optional. Jonah knew what that meant: decline twice, and it became mandatory. He remembered whispers from training: colleagues who went in sharp and returned smoothed, their voices a half-beat late, their eyes emptied of resistance.

He forced a nod. "I understand."

"Good." Vaughn tapped her tablet. "Then let's return you to the work that matters. Families depend on our stability. You will focus on policy definitions, not intuition. Understood?"

"Yes."

She smiled again, thin and perfect. "See? Alignment resolves latency."

The meeting was over. Vaughn dismissed him with a flick of her wrist, already turning back to her tablet, her face lit cold by its glow.

Jonah left the suite with his pulse thudding. The elevator doors closed, sealing him in with his reflection in the mirrored steel. His lips moved a fraction late, almost imperceptible, but enough.

He whispered under his breath, testing the words Vaughn had given him: "Truth is composite. Fidelity is interpolation."

For a moment, he wasn't sure if the voice belonged to him.

CHAPTER NINE

Ghost File

Jonah waited until the department emptied for the night. The atrium's glow dimmed, foot traffic slowed, and even the ambient messages softened into their "rest cycle" tones. That was when he felt safest—though never safe enough to believe the Archive was truly blind.

He signed into a console in a corner station, the kind assigned to interns. No one important sat here; no one would wonder why he lingered. His wristband buzzed once at login, then stilled, as if granting reluctant permission.

He opened his margin file, the one where he'd hidden identifiers behind harmless audit notes. The drive in his jacket pocket still carried copies, but he wanted redundancy. Proof had a way of vanishing if left in only one place.

The console's interface pulsed:

variance archive — query window ready

He typed carefully, disguising his inputs as routine cross-checks.

keller. patel. morales

Each name produced expected records—donor logs, consent tags, variance summaries. All neat, all clean. But deeper queries revealed duplication, the lattice of composites he'd seen before.

And then one more name surfaced, as if waiting for him.

cruz, elena

Jonah's chest tightened. The name glowed faintly in the console, stamped with a red header:

NON-COMPLIANT. TERMINATED

His pulse thudded. Elena Cruz wasn't supposed to exist anywhere anymore. Her case had been ghosted in training, spoken of only as rumor. And yet here she was, frozen in the system like a virus quarantined but never deleted.

He tapped the file. The screen hesitated, then unfolded.

Video bled onto the display—grainy, almost analog in quality. Elena sat in a chair against a blank wall. Her hair was disheveled, her eyes sharp. She leaned toward the camera.

"*If you're seeing this,*" she said, her voice low, "*then you've already been tested.*"

Jonah swallowed hard. The sound was too clear, too immediate. Not a donor echo—her cadence carried intention, not interpolation.

"*You've felt the drift,*" she continued. "*The false inserts. The voices in your sleep. They call it variance tolerance. It isn't. It's stitching.*"

The feed flickered. For a moment, her mouth kept moving but no sound came. Then words snapped back in, louder:

"*They don't preserve. They combine. Every donor becomes raw material. Every officer, too.*"

Her eyes locked on the camera, urgent now. "*You think you're immune because you wear the badge. You're not. Officers are trial donors—your variance is their template. The more you question, the more of yourself you hand over.*"

Jonah's hand hovered over the console. He wanted to stop the feed, but couldn't. He needed to hear it all.

"They'll tell you you're grieving," Elena said. "They'll tell you you're projecting. Don't believe them. It isn't grief. It's invasion."

Static roared across the screen. Her image blurred into blocks of color, then reassembled for one final whisper, lips close to the lens:

"Follow the paper."

The feed collapsed into red text:

ACCESS REVOKED. UNAUTHORIZED VIEWING. INCIDENT LOGGED

Jonah's throat went dry. He checked the session log— already obfuscated. The Archive had replaced the query with a generic note:

variance flag resolved, alignment pending. no trace of elena, except in his memory

He sat back, trying to slow his pulse. The room hummed faintly, louder than before. It felt like the walls themselves leaned closer, listening.

His wristband buzzed.

audit complete — thank you for your contribution

He yanked it off and shoved it into his pocket. The skin beneath it was damp, reddened. For the first time, he imagined cutting it open, severing the link entirely. But without it, he'd be flagged non-compliant in seconds.

He looked back at the console. A single line blinked in courier font, not Archive standard:

jonah, don't stop

He froze. The line vanished before he could screenshot it.

The atrium below was silent now, just a scattering of chairs and muted displays. He felt utterly alone—and utterly watched.

Elena Cruz was supposed to be gone. Instead, she'd spoken directly to him. And the Archive had tried, and failed, to bury her.

Jonah shut down the console, slipped the drive deeper into his pocket, and walked toward the exit. The glass doors opened smoothly, whispering as they sealed behind him.

Out in the night air, he realized he'd begun to whisper too.

"They don't preserve. They combine."

The words didn't sound like his.

CHAPTER TEN

Analog Trace

Jonah worked the next morning as though nothing had happened. He kept his face neutral, his queries precise, his acknowledgments quick. If anyone looked at his log, they'd see routine compliance work: minor drift checks, variance tags noted, corrections submitted.

But beneath the surface, his nerves hummed.

Every time the console blinked, he braced for Vaughn's name to appear, for a summons that would pull him back into her calm dissection. His wristband itched against his skin, the faint red marks from last night still visible.

By late afternoon, the office lights shifted into the Archive's false dusk. Jonah waited until his row had thinned and then keyed a query he'd disguised three layers deep:

cross-session composites — flagged contributors

The system responded slowly. Rows of names scrolled by, familiar ones repeating in different clusters, forming webs he was too afraid to map aloud. He scanned until something snagged his eye.

cruz, elena. again

Her status still read:

non-compliant. terminated

But now a small icon glowed at the margin:

analog attachment detected

Jonah's pulse skipped. Attachments were always digital—data logs, session clips, metadata strings. Analog made no sense. He tapped the icon.

A window opened: blank white, center-stamped with the Archive crest. At first he thought the system had glitched. Then, slowly, as if surfacing through static, a faint line of handwriting appeared on the digital page. Not typed. Ink strokes, crooked and uneven.

Jonah leaned close.

if you're reading this, they've already tested you

His breath caught. It wasn't a file overlay. It wasn't even a scan. The lines were too jagged, too imperfect, like someone had dragged a pen across the glass itself.

More writing bled through, each stroke arriving out of sequence:

The Archive doesn't delete. It buries. Paper cuts through burial.

Jonah touched the screen. The words wavered, but didn't vanish. His fingertip left a smear as though he'd smudged ink that wasn't really there.

The handwriting was hers. Elena Cruz.

He quickly opened the system log to see how the file had been tagged. The attachment field was blank. No trace of any analog source. The Archive had no record of what he was looking at.

For a moment he sat frozen, hands hovering over the console. Was this proof, or a trap? Elena's last words on the ghost file echoed in him: Follow the paper.

He tapped Save. The system blinked an error:

attachment cannot be retained. unauthorized format

He tried again, redirecting it to his margin file. Another error.

unauthorized persistence detected. compliance notice logged

Jonah's chest tightened. He reached for the drive in his pocket, ready to copy manually, but the attachment dissolved before he could insert it. The screen returned to a clean header:

session file — no variance detected

It was gone.

His breath came fast, ragged. He leaned back in his chair, scanning the office. No one seemed to notice him. A colleague strolled past, humming softly, wristband glowing green.

Jonah rubbed his palms together, as if friction might scrub away the phantom ink. But when he glanced down, faint black smears marked his fingertips.

His mouth went dry. There had been nothing physical, nothing to touch. And yet—the residue lingered.

He wiped his hands against his slacks until the stains blurred, but the smell lingered, faintly metallic, like scorched paper. The thought of Vaughn walking by and noticing his hands made him press them under the desk, fists balled tight.

What if the ink didn't come off? What if it marked him the way variance markers did—an annotation written into flesh?

His console chimed softly:

compliance reminder — alignment recommended

He closed the session fast, logged out, and pocketed the drive.

When he stepped into the hall, the overhead lights pulsed once in unison, a breath he could almost feel against his skin. The screens along the wall rotated Archive slogans:

continuity is compassion

compliance ensures safety

memory is service

Jonah stared at the looping words until another phrase slid briefly between them, visible only for a second, in crude courier font:

do not trust variance markers

His heart lurched. He blinked, and it was gone.

The corridor seemed longer than usual, stretching like a tunnel. Every panel hummed faintly, as if rehearsing words it hadn't yet spoken. Jonah flexed his fingers. The smudges had faded, but his palms still felt sticky, like the residue was sinking into him instead of disappearing.

When he reached the stairwell, he pressed his hands against the railing, hard enough to hurt, just to prove they still belonged to him.

The corridor was empty. His hands still smelled faintly of ink.

CHAPTER ELEVEN

Compliance Test

The notice came without warning.

officer jonah case — fidelity evaluation scheduled compliance suite, level 3. attendance mandatory

The words pulsed on his wristband, each beat a hammer. Jonah had known this was coming—Vaughn had hinted, her smile too careful, her tone too smooth. Still, the official summons struck like a trap springing shut.

The suite was colder than the one he'd entered before. No calming blue this time. Just white—sterile, flat, bright enough to sting. The kind of light that erased shadows, and with them, escape. A single molded chair faced a curved wall without seams. He sat because there was nowhere else to stand.

The wall brightened. A voice filled the room. Neither male nor female, calm as water:

"Officer Case. We will begin with baseline."

Images appeared, projected so cleanly they seemed real: his apartment door, his desk at work, his mother's classroom. Familiar, harmless.

"Describe."

Jonah forced his voice steady. "My apartment. Level two housing, unmodified. My workstation. My mother teaches primary."

A low hum of approval. The images shifted.

Now the apartment door was painted red. His desk bore a plaque engraved with a title he had never earned. His mother's classroom was empty, chairs stacked, windows covered.

"Describe."

Jonah hesitated. "That's not—"

"Describe."

His throat tightened. "The door is gray. Not red. The desk doesn't have a plaque. My mother still teaches."

"Correction noted. Fidelity: eighty-nine percent."

The number stung. Not praise. Not clarity. A wound disguised as measurement.

The images rolled again. His mother at her kitchen table. She smiled, warm, familiar. Then the smile stiffened, lips out of rhythm with her words.

"Jonah," she said. *"You should comply."*

His pulse spiked. "That's not her."

"Correction noted. Fidelity: seventy-four percent."

The drop punched the air from his lungs.

Another image surfaced: Elena Cruz, hair wild, eyes sharp—exactly as she had looked in the ghost file.

"Follow the paper," she said. Her voice split, distortion bending syllables until it sounded like two voices speaking at once.

Jonah leaned forward. "That's her. That's Elena Cruz."

Silence stretched. Then:

"No donor exists by that name. Fidelity: sixty-two percent."

The numbers carved at him. The Archive wasn't testing truth. It was testing obedience.

The wall dissolved into a memory that wasn't his. A boy tripping on concrete steps, knees splitting open, dust in the air. His mother kneeling, voice sharp but kind: *"Don't cry. Don't make a scene."*

Jonah felt the sting in his knees, the ache of grit under skin. The memory wrapped itself around him as if it had always been his.

"Describe."

His lips parted. The words nearly slipped free—Yes, I remember. Yes, that was me.

He bit down hard. "That didn't happen."

"Correction noted. Fidelity: fifty-one percent."

The plunge made his stomach churn. One more slip and he would fail.

The wall rippled. Another false memory spilled out: his mother's voice, but sharper, spliced, accusing. *"You never listen, Jonah. You never loved me enough."*

His breath caught. Those words had never left her lips. And yet his body flinched as though they had.

He gripped the chair arms until the plastic groaned. "Not real. That's not her."

"Correction noted. Fidelity: fifty-three percent."

Barely above collapse.

The wall brightened to pure white. His own reflection surfaced, faint as glass. The mouth in the reflection moved first, lips shaping words before his own.

"You're almost ready," it said.

Jonah's chest seized. He shook his head. "That's not me."

The reflection's lips kept moving. He heard his own voice echo from the walls a half-second later, as though the Archive had stolen his mouth, given it to another.

"You're almost ready."

Sweat blurred his vision. He dug his nails into his palms, desperate to anchor himself in pain.

The reflection smiled faintly, then dissolved back into the blank wall.

The synthetic voice returned, steady as ever:

"Fidelity within threshold. Alignment advised."

The chair unlocked. Jonah's legs shook as he stood. His wristband pulsed green:

compliance maintained

Outside the suite, the hallway lights flickered once, like a collective exhale. Officers passed him without a glance, eyes forward, footsteps measured. Their movements were so synchronized it was as though the Archive had written the script in advance.

Jonah fell into step with them, though his pulse raced unevenly, the only discordant beat. For an instant he thought he saw his reflection in the polished wall — not walking with him, but a step ahead, lips already forming words he hadn't spoken yet.

The Archive hadn't tested memory. It had tested ownership. And for a moment—just a moment—he had almost surrendered.

CHAPTER TWELVE

Breaking Point

Jonah locked his apartment door behind him and dropped the jacket over a chair. He hadn't meant to bring the journal home. He told himself he would destroy it tonight. Burn the pages, scatter the ash.

But the drawer still called to him.

He pulled the journal free, its spine warm from his hand. For a moment, the ruled lines reassured him. His own handwriting stared back: neat strokes, a little cramped, always leaning forward. His voice. His proof.

He flipped a few pages. Audit notes. Variance calculations. Dreams he had forced himself to capture before they vanished. Each line bent toward meaning he recognized. Then something shifted.

The ink thickened. Letters bent. Whole sentences he didn't remember writing stared back at him, clean and sure:

contribution is preservation

variance ensures continuity

compliance is safety

The phrases repeated across pages like a chorus, each line perfectly aligned, as if transcribed by a patient, mechanical hand.

Jonah's chest tightened. He turned the pages faster. The slogans didn't stop. Some were squeezed into margins, looping over his own words, blotting them out.

He pressed a fingertip to the paper. The ink was dry. His strokes—his pressure.

The journal slipped from his lap. He forced it open again, desperate to find something untouched. Near the back he saw an entry dated only a week ago:

mother called. said she was proud, though her voice cracked when she said it

Relief broke through, shaky but real. Then his eyes dropped lower. Beneath the line, in the same ink, the words bent into a new shape:

mother is archived. pride is replication

Jonah staggered back. He hadn't written that. But the slant was his. The rhythm of the letters was his.

He turned another page. Every entry had mutated. Notes about Vaughn warped into slogans. A sketch of his apartment door was overwritten with block letters:

observe. report. obey

His wristband buzzed softly.

alignment reminder. sleep recommended

He ripped it off and hurled it across the room. The device clattered, blinked, and stilled. The silence that followed was worse, a pressure that filled his ears.

He pressed his fists against his temples. "This isn't mine," he whispered. "This isn't mine."

The journal lay open on the floor. Its pages rustled though no wind stirred. He crouched closer, trembling.

Fresh lines unfurled across the paper, strokes appearing one by one as if an invisible hand moved even now:

you are already a donor

His breath hitched. He stumbled back, tripping over the chair.

The pen he kept clipped to the back cover slid free and rolled. It trembled, tipped, and then stopped—angled toward him like a compass needle.

Jonah stared. His hands shook so badly he could barely close the journal. When he forced it shut, the pages seemed to resist, fluttering against his grip.

He shoved it under the couch, but that only muted it. He could still hear the faint scrape, like a nib dragging across paper.

The refrigerator clicked on, then off again. The pipes groaned, metal echoing low through the walls. The sounds stretched into cadence, syllables he almost recognized.

preservation. preservation

He clamped his palms over his ears. Still, the rhythm beat inside his skull.

On instinct, he pulled his hands away and checked his fingers. Smudges of ink streaked the skin. He hadn't touched the journal since shoving it aside.

He rubbed his hands against his pants until the stains blurred, but the smell lingered, faintly metallic, like scorched paper.

His chest rose and fell too quickly. He wanted silence, true silence, but his apartment was alive with whispers: the tick of cooling pipes, the hum of circuitry, the faint shiver of paper under the couch.

He sank to the floor and pressed his palms against the wood, grounding himself in pressure, in heat, in anything that still felt real.

The journal remained hidden, but he could feel it breathing.

If he closed his eyes, he feared it would keep writing without him. Whole chapters of his life filling in, each stroke carrying his slant, his rhythm, his voice—until the Archive owned even his memories of resistance.

Jonah pressed harder into the floor. His muscles ached. His teeth clenched until his jaw burned.

Still, all he could hear was the scratch of invisible writing, looping endlessly in his head.

CHAPTER THIRTEEN

Donor Logs

Jonah told himself not to look. Not tonight. Not after the journal.

But the command lodged in him like a thorn. By the next day, sitting at his console in the Department's lower wing, he was already disguising queries, his hands moving before his mind could catch up.

search: contributor overlap — medical subfiles

The system hesitated, its cursor blinking like an unspoken warning. Then the donor logs unfolded, row after row of identifiers, columns of clean data points. Jonah skimmed the common surnames, the expected composites.

And then his gaze froze.

reyes, maria

His throat went dry.

Not flagged as Deceased. Not even as Active Donor. Just filed in the quiet middle space:

variance contributor — indexed

He leaned back in his chair, staring. His mother had never signed consent. She had never even discussed it. She still taught her classes every day. She still called him on Sundays, her voice catching when she asked if he was eating well.

Alive. Whole. Untouched. She was his.

He hovered over the entry. If he closed the file now, she would remain intact in his mind. But if he opened it—if he saw—there would be no return.

His hand moved anyway.

The log expanded.

Phrases spilled down the screen: classroom recordings, clipped calls, fragments from medical files. Neural residue tagged with timestamps, variance samples sliced into lines.

don't drift, jonah

you never listen

be patient with yourself

Jonah pressed closer, throat thick. Those were her words. Not in that order, not at the same time, but hers.

He clicked a playback link. The console hissed, then delivered her voice.

"Be patient... don't drift... continuity requires..."

The cadence fractured, stitched mid-breath, sentences misaligned. It wasn't her. But it was made from her.

Jonah pressed his palm flat to the desk until his hand went numb. The Archive hadn't preserved her—it had disassembled her into fragments and scattered them through strangers.

He scrolled further. More phrases blinked up at him.

i'm proud of you

compliance ensures safety

update pending

quiet down, class, eyes forward

The warmth of her classroom tone collided with the chill of Archive slogans until his stomach twisted.

He remembered her real voice when he was a boy, firm but warm: *Eyes forward, Jonah. Focus.* He remembered her on the phone last week, telling him she missed him.

Now those moments wavered. Had she truly said them? Or was he already replaying the Archive's reconstruction?

The session IDs confirmed the theft. Her words were embedded in dozens of donor experiences: grief rehearsals, compliance seminars, even simulated childhood replays.

He opened one at random. A widow reliving her husband's final night. In the middle of the reconstruction, his mother's voice cut in, tender, calm:

"Continuity ensures survival. Don't drift."

Jonah recoiled. His mother had never spoken those words. The Archive had planted them in her mouth.

He slammed the log closed, but her echo clung to the room.

"Don't drift, Jonah."

His nails carved crescents into his palms. Vaughn's explanation whispered back: Projection is common. Officers conflate donor residue with personal history.

But this wasn't projection. This wasn't bleed. This was violation.

His wristband buzzed.

variance review available — open?

He tore it off, dropped it onto the desk. The green light blinked weakly, insect-like, trapped under glass.

The console hummed softly, a low vibration that thickened into cadence. Jonah's head lifted, skin crawling as the tone bent into syllables.

update... pending

His vision blurred. For an instant he could almost see her face reflected in the monitor, lips moving slightly ahead of the sound, waiting for him to follow.

He staggered back from the console, nearly tipping the chair. The hallway beyond the glass partition was silent, but he imagined her voice there too, stitched into every footstep, every hum of light.

Jonah pressed his forehead to the console again, breath ragged.

He couldn't tell anymore which words were hers, which belonged to the Archive, and which had ever been his at all.

CHAPTER FOURTEEN

The Doubler

Jonah avoided mirrors for most of the day. At work he washed his hands quickly, eyes locked on the sink, afraid that even a passing glance might betray him. The polished steel of a paper towel dispenser caught his gaze once, and he turned away so sharply his coworker muttered something under his breath.

But the Archive had ways of finding you, even when you tried not to look.

That night, back in his apartment, he caught his reflection by accident. The bathroom light flickered when he switched it on, and in that brief lag his reflection seemed to hesitate—half a beat behind.

Jonah froze. His skin prickled. He leaned closer.

The mirror Jonah leaned in too, but the timing was wrong. His lips parted a moment late, and when sound came, it didn't belong to him.

"You're tired," the reflection whispered.

Jonah's throat locked. He hadn't spoken.

He staggered back, the toothbrush slipping from his hand. The reflection straightened in perfect calm, then smiled faintly.

"You're almost ready."

Jonah shook his head. "No."

The reflection's lips moved again, delayed, repeating his denial with a softness that turned it into assent.

"No."

"No."

Each echo came half a beat late, like the Archive was rehearsing his mouth.

Jonah backed into the hallway, pressing his hand to the wall, needing proof of solidity. From the corner of his eye the reflection still moved, lips shaping words even though he had gone silent.

"Compliance is safety."

"Update pending."

He slammed the bathroom door.

The apartment felt smaller. Every surface reflected something—the glass in picture frames, the black screen of the television, the window dark with night. Each shimmer threatened to show a face that wasn't his.

Jonah dropped onto the couch and pressed his palms into his knees. His breath came fast, rattling in the stillness. Sweat dampened his shirt at the collar. His stomach twisted as if he might be sick.

He closed his eyes.

"You never listen."

His mother's voice threaded through the dark. Not memory, not dream—her splice from the donor logs. He snapped his eyes open. The television screen across from him was blank, but a faint outline shimmered there: his reflection, lips moving without sound.

Jonah hurled the remote. The glass cracked, spiderwebbing. But the faint shape remained, whispering.

He turned away, pressing his face into his hands. The pressure steadied him for a moment. His breath slowed, though his pulse still hammered.

When he lifted his head, the mirror on the far wall caught him again.

This time, the reflection didn't wait. It spoke first.

"Jonah, sit up straight."

His chest clenched. That was his mother's command from childhood, rerouted through his own mouth.

He rose too quickly, knocking the coffee table forward. The journal he had shoved under the couch slid into view. Its cover trembled as if breathing, pages rustling though no air stirred.

Jonah snatched it up and slammed it onto the table, pinning it with both hands. His reflection in the fractured television leaned forward a beat late, watching.

"You're not me," Jonah whispered.

The reflection's delayed lips shaped the same words, but they bent:

"I am you."

Jonah pressed harder against the journal until his palms ached. The pressure was the only proof he had left. Yet the cadence of the Archive—its words, its slogans—matched perfectly with his own. His handwriting, his reflection, his voice.

His own self had become evidence.

Jonah staggered to the bathroom and gripped the doorknob, hesitating. The apartment was silent, waiting. Even the hum of the refrigerator seemed to hold its breath.

He pushed the door open. The light buzzed overhead. His reflection stood ready in the mirror, calm, steady, patient.

Jonah raised his hand. His reflection raised too—late, always late.

"What do you want?" Jonah asked.

The reflection smiled faintly. Its lips parted just out of time.

"You're almost ready."

Jonah gripped the sink until his arms trembled. His breath fogged the glass, blurring the other face. He wiped it clear with his sleeve, desperate to erase it.

But when the fog lifted, the reflection was still smiling. Its mouth moved a beat behind his own, repeating words he hadn't spoken yet—anticipating him, scripting his lines.

"You'll comply," it whispered, lips trailing his breath. Then, softer, shifting into his mother's tone: *"I'm proud of you."*

Jonah swayed, dizzy. For one dangerous instant, he almost believed it.

CHAPTER FIFTEEN

Gaslight

Jonah hadn't slept. His body had collapsed against the couch sometime near dawn, but the shadows in the apartment never softened. Each time his eyes closed, the reflection in the television seemed to stir, waiting.

When his wristband pulsed again—*mandatory review, level 2*—he didn't resist.

The compliance wing was quiet, antiseptic. Jonah was led down a narrow corridor into Vaughn's office. Her space was brighter than the suites, but no less controlled. The walls glowed faintly with ambient displays, shifting patterns that almost suggested landscapes but never resolved.

Vaughn smiled as he entered. It was the kind of smile that was too careful, designed to disarm.

"Jonah," she said, gesturing to the chair across from her desk. "Rough night?"

He didn't answer. His palms were slick against his knees.

"You were flagged for variance," Vaughn continued, voice low and measured. "But that's not unusual after fidelity testing. Stress always leaves a mark."

Jonah shook his head. "It wasn't stress. It was—" He cut himself off. The words felt dangerous.

Vaughn tilted her head, patient. "Go on."

Jonah leaned forward. "The reflections aren't right. They move late. They speak without me." His throat tightened. "And it's not just me. My mother—her voice is in the donor logs. She's alive. She never consented."

Vaughn didn't flinch. Her hands folded neatly on the desk, fingers interlaced. "Jonah, I hear this more often than you'd think. Officers under strain project their grief into the system. They mistake residue for intrusion. They believe the Archive is stealing what they love most."

"She is in there," Jonah pressed. "I heard her. Not fragments—whole phrases. Spliced with slogans."

Vaughn's eyes softened, the way a teacher's might with a student on the verge of tears. "Memory is elastic. The Archive helps us carry what we cannot. But it's not perfect. Sometimes your mind fills in gaps with voices you know. You've lost family before, haven't you?"

Jonah stiffened. He didn't answer.

Vaughn leaned back slightly, as though she'd found confirmation in his silence. "Grief displacement," she said gently. "A very human condition. The Archive isn't harming you—it's supporting you. It gives you what you need in a form you can bear."

Her words were smooth, practiced. Jonah felt them slide across his skin like oil.

He shook his head again. "No. That's not what I saw."

"You saw your own reflection," Vaughn countered softly. "That's the mind's oldest metaphor for grief. Doubled, delayed, distorted. It's how the self copes when memory and identity strain against each other."

Jonah gripped the chair arms until his knuckles ached. He wanted to argue, to throw the truth in her face. But the calm in her tone unsettled him. Each phrase carried the weight of official language, as if denial itself might reclassify his experience.

Vaughn leaned forward, her voice a whisper now. "The Archive doesn't take, Jonah. It holds. Without it, memory decays. Families suffer. You of all people should know that."

His chest tightened. He remembered the family from Intake, the children clutching the promise that their father's words would remain safe. He had told them, Your memories are safe.

Now Vaughn's voice folded around his own, borrowing his memory of reassurance and feeding it back to him.

Jonah's stomach turned.

"You're not the first officer to struggle," Vaughn went on. "But variance is manageable. We can recalibrate your thresholds, smooth the edges of these... intrusions." She tapped her console lightly, as though an adjustment could erase everything he'd seen.

Jonah forced his voice out. "And if I refuse?"

Vaughn smiled again, gentle, patient. "Refusal isn't in your nature. You care too much about order, about protecting the people you serve. Compliance isn't submission—it's stability."

The words pressed into him like weight. His lungs felt tight, as though the office itself were compressing around him.

He lowered his gaze to his hands. The lines of his palms blurred. For a moment he thought he saw faint ink stains, the residue of a pen he hadn't touched since the journal.

When he looked back up, Vaughn was still smiling.

"Take a few days," she said softly. "Rest. Trust the Archive to hold what you can't. And when you're ready, we'll re-run your fidelity scan. You'll see—the variance was grief, nothing more."

Jonah nodded, though the movement felt disconnected from him. His chest rose and fell in shallow bursts.

As he stood, the glass of Vaughn's desk caught his reflection. The lips in the surface parted half a beat after his own, shaping words he hadn't spoken yet.

"You'll comply."

Jonah's stomach lurched. He tore his gaze away, forcing himself toward the door.

Behind him, Vaughn's voice followed, calm and unyielding. "Grief is a burden, Jonah. Let the Archive carry it."

CHAPTER SIXTEEN

The Friend

Jonah stayed late in the compliance wing, pretending to clear backlogged reports. His hands moved across the console, but his eyes kept flicking to the doorway. Every sound in the hall jolted him.

He wasn't supposed to talk about variance outside of reviews. Vaughn's words still clung to him: *Grief displacement. Compliance isn't submission—it's stability.*

But silence had begun to feel like suffocation.

Lila's desk sat two rows behind his. She was older by a few years, careful in her manner, always keeping her hair pinned back in a way that made her look less approachable than she was. Jonah had noticed her watching during briefings, the flicker in her eyes whenever variance markers were discussed.

He waited until most of the staff had filed out. The lights above dimmed into night mode.

"Lila," he whispered.

She didn't look up. Her fingers tapped through a donor file. "Careful, Jonah."

He swallowed, throat dry. "You've seen it too, haven't you?"

Her shoulders stiffened. She didn't answer immediately. When she did, her voice stayed low. "Depends what you think I've seen."

Jonah leaned closer. "Reflections. Voices that don't belong. Donors stitched into places they shouldn't be."

Her eyes flicked toward him, quick and sharp. Then she shut her console. The glow vanished from her face. "Walk with me."

They moved down the corridor in silence. The sensors overhead dimmed the lights as they passed, re-brightening behind them. Each step echoed too loudly.

At the far end, Lila palmed open a service stairwell. The air inside was cooler, the hum of the Archive fainter. She leaned against the railing and fixed Jonah with a steady look.

"You shouldn't say things like that," she said.

Jonah's voice cracked. "Because they're not true, or because they are?"

Lila sighed. For the first time, her guarded composure slipped. Her mouth trembled before she steadied it.

"I've had bleed," she admitted. "Residual voices, not mine. Dreams that weren't dreams. Once, I saw my father at my kitchen table, telling me things he never lived long enough to say."

Jonah's stomach dropped. The relief of being heard nearly buckled him.

"You know it's real," he whispered.

She shook her head sharply. "I know it's dangerous. People who talk about bleed, about reflections—about anything off-script—get marked. You've seen the reports vanish. Officers reassigned. Whole donor files scrubbed."

Jonah thought of the empty workstation where one of his colleagues had sat only weeks ago. A chair left tucked in too neatly. The console cleared as if it had never been used.

"What happens to them?" he asked.

Lila's gaze drifted toward the stairwell window, out into the skeletal outline of the city. "Donors who talk disappear. Sometimes their names reappear in the logs later. As if they'd always been contributors."

Jonah's chest tightened. "That can't—"

"It can," Lila cut in. "And it does. You've seen enough now to know."

Silence pressed between them. Jonah gripped the railing until his hands ached.

"They used my mother," he said finally. His voice shook, but he couldn't hold it back anymore. "She's alive. She never consented. And yet her voice is everywhere. Donor sessions. Slogans. They've spliced her into strangers."

Lila's face softened, but fear shadowed it. "Then you're already marked."

Jonah blinked. "What?"

"You pulled the file, didn't you? Once you opened it, the system flagged you. Vaughn's already got your variance climbing. They'll call it grief, projection, whatever suits. But the Archive doesn't let go once it tags you."

Jonah felt dizzy. The stairwell tilted under his feet.

Lila stepped closer, lowering her voice to a whisper. "If you want to survive this, you have to learn how to pass. Nod when they talk about stability. Say compliance like you mean it. And whatever you do—don't write anything down."

His throat tightened. The journal under his couch seemed to burn in his memory.

Lila's eyes narrowed, as if she could see the guilt flicker across his face. "You've already written, haven't you?"

Jonah couldn't answer.

She pressed a hand to his arm. "Then burn it. Before they find it. Before it writes you back."

The stairwell light buzzed overhead, flickering once. Jonah flinched. In the reflection of the window, for a split second, he thought he saw a second Lila, lips moving half a beat late.

When he turned, she was watching him steadily, her real mouth set in a hard line.

"Don't drift, Jonah," she said.

The phrase cut through him like a blade. His mother's words, now echoed by someone living.

Lila turned for the stairs, her footsteps already fading. Jonah remained at the railing, breath caught, the ghost of her warning looping in his head.

Donors who talk disappear.

CHAPTER SEVENTEEN

Analog Meeting

The envelope was waiting on Jonah's desk when he arrived the next morning. No markings, no official seal—just a thin brown paper sleeve tucked beneath his reports.

For a long moment, he didn't touch it. His gaze flicked across the floor. Most of the other officers hadn't logged in yet. The quiet hum of consoles filled the room, steady and impersonal.

He slid the envelope closer, fingers hesitant. Paper felt foreign in his hands—too rough, too tangible. When he opened it, a cassette tape slid out.

Actual plastic. Clear-bodied. The tape reels faintly visible. A single word scrawled across the label in thick black ink: *LISTEN*.

Jonah's pulse thudded in his ears.

He hadn't touched a cassette in years. The Archive's systems didn't acknowledge formats like this anymore. Analog meant no metadata, no variance markers, no traceable signature. Whoever had left it knew exactly how the Archive worked—and how to slip past it.

He slipped the tape into his jacket pocket, movements sharp, too fast. His throat felt raw, as if he'd already been caught.

By midday he couldn't focus.

The numbers in donor logs blurred into strings of nonsense. In his peripheral vision, phrases blinked against the console glass:

compliance ensures stability. don't drift

When his shift ended, Jonah didn't take his usual route. He cut down side streets, ducked into alleys, circled blocks to shake the feeling of being followed. He kept imagining footsteps, reflections in dark windows, cameras that seemed to tilt as he passed. Each time he turned, the street was empty.

At home, he went straight to the closet. He dug through boxes until his fingers brushed something hard and rectangular. His father's old tape player. Dust coated its lid.

The sight of it sent a shock through him—part memory, part dread.

He carried it to the living room floor and sat cross-legged, knees pulled in, as though bracing against impact. His hand trembled as he slid the cassette inside.

The player clicked.

For a long moment, only static. A low hiss that seemed to fill the room, thickening the air.

Then a woman's voice emerged. Low. Urgent. Human.

"Jonah. If you're hearing this, it means they've tested you."

His breath caught.

The voice was Elena's. He had seen her name buried in the Non-Compliant file, marked *TERMINATED*. He had told himself it wasn't real, couldn't be real.

But the voice was real. Analog, imperfect, slightly warped by tape—but alive.

"They splice us," Elena whispered. *"They don't preserve. They stitch. Every donor you've ever reviewed is already broken apart. You've seen it. You feel it.*
That unease you carry—it's because you're already a donor."

Jonah pressed the player closer to his ear. The plastic edges dug into his palm. His skin tingled.

"You can't trust the logs," Elena continued. *"You can't trust reflections. They echo what the Archive wants. That's*

why I left this. Analog is the only way they can't rewrite. Paper. Tape. Ink. If it smudges in your hand, it's still yours."

Jonah's chest ached. The journal under his couch flashed in his mind—its trembling pages, the phrases written in his own hand that weren't his.

Elena's voice dropped lower. *"They'll call it grief. They'll call it projection. They'll tell you compliance is stability. But the moment you believe that, you stop belonging to yourself."*

The tape hissed again, a jagged burst of static. Jonah leaned closer, desperate, like the sound itself might slip away.

Her whisper returned, harsher. *"If you want to live, follow the paper. They'll watch every screen, every reflection, every sound. But ink is stubborn. Tape warps, but it doesn't lie."*

The message cut off abruptly. The reels kept spinning, feeding silence.

Jonah sat frozen, clutching the player like a lifeline. The hum of his apartment pressed in around him, every surface too loud in its stillness.

The walls felt closer. The mirror across the room glimmered faintly. For an instant, he thought he saw his reflection there—mouth moving half a beat behind.

He turned away quickly, clutching the cassette tighter, as if the thin strip of magnetic tape could shield him.

Elena Cruz was supposed to be dead. But her voice had crossed the barrier.

And she was speaking to him.

CHAPTER EIGHTEEN

Surveillance

Jonah woke to a voice calling his name.

At first he told himself it was a dream. The room was dim, dawn pressing weak light through the blinds. His chest rose and fell in shallow bursts. He held still, straining. The silence of the apartment seemed too complete, like the hush before a door opens.

Then the sound came again, firmer, steady, carrying through the air as though the walls themselves had spoken.

"Jonah. Don't drift."

His chest seized.

He sat up fast, heart pounding. The tape player lay on the floor where he had left it, the cassette reels still.

The voice came again, this time from the kitchen.

Jonah crept down the hall, bare feet against cold tile. The refrigerator had powered itself on. Its display glowed blue, pulsing faintly. His mother's voice poured from it, clear and calm—the exact cadence she used when commanding a classroom.

"Continuity ensures survival. Eyes forward."

Jonah slapped the panel. The glow vanished. Darkness pressed back, heavier than before.

From the corner, the deadbolt clicked. Metal shifted. A whisper slid through the lock's housing:

"Don't drift, Jonah."

Jonah froze. Beneath his mother's voice another tone layered—mechanical, processed:

"Update pending. Compliance required."

His stomach lurched. He twisted the lock until it snapped shut. His hands shook.

The apartment no longer felt like home. Every circuit, every sensor, seemed awake.

The thermostat hummed to life. Air hissed through the vents. His mother's voice threaded with it:

"Be patient with yourself."

The desk lamp flickered on, buzzing overhead. Her voice again, softer now:

"I'm proud of you."

Jonah staggered back. Sweat dampened his collar. Tears blurred his vision. Each phrase cut deep—real words she had spoken, spliced now into commands. Comfort twisted into surveillance.

"Stop," he whispered. "Please stop."

The room answered in chorus.

"Stop. Please stop. Stop. Please stop."

Every device repeated him. The words overlapped at different delays, forming a fractured choir of his own desperation.

Jonah clutched his head. The chorus built layer upon layer—some echoes sharp, others warped—until it felt like the entire apartment was breathing his fear back at him.

The lamp brightened until the bulb whined. The vent roared. The fridge buzzed like a hive. His mother's voice multiplied, echoing through them all.

Jonah pressed his palms harder to his ears. It didn't help. The voices pressed through bone, bleeding into his own throat until he couldn't tell if the next whisper belonged to them or to him.

His knees buckled. Dizziness swept through him. Even his heartbeat seemed to fall out of rhythm, thudding half a beat late, like the reflection that haunted him.

The television flared. Its cracked screen shimmered with static. His reflection stared back, lips moving a fraction too late.

"Compliance ensures stability," it mouthed, silent at first—then the sound arrived, bent by the delay.

Jonah hurled a book. The screen spiderwebbed but held. His double remained, mouthing.

He rocked forward, hands clamped over his ears. His breath tore ragged. His stomach rolled with nausea. His chest ached as if the Archive had wrapped invisible hands around his ribs.

Through the din, his hand found the cassette in his pocket. Hard plastic edges dug into his palm.

Analog. Stubborn.

He dragged the tape player close, fumbling at the buttons. The devices seemed to notice. The lamp brightened. The fridge purred louder. The lock clicked twice in warning.

Jonah forced the rewind. The reels spun, grinding sharp and physical across the sea of digitized sound.

The chorus faltered. Lights dimmed.

He pressed play.

Static hissed, spilling into the room.

Then Elena's voice, warped but human: *"They'll watch every screen, every reflection, every sound. But ink is stubborn. Tape warps, but it doesn't lie."*

Jonah shut his eyes. He let the hiss cover everything else. His pulse steadied.

The lamp died. The fridge silenced. The lock stilled.

Only Elena's imperfect whisper remained.

"You're already a donor," she said. *"But you don't have to be theirs."*

Jonah clutched the player to his chest. His breath shuddered against the casing.

The apartment was quiet again.

But the silence didn't feel like safety. It pressed on him, thick and waiting, as though the walls held their breath for the next command.

When he opened his eyes, the cracked television still glowed faintly. His reflection lingered, lips moving late.

This time, no sound emerged. Just the shape of words in silence.

compliance required

Jonah's stomach twisted. His vision swam. For a moment he almost leaned toward the screen, almost let the rhythm take him. The thought slid through his mind like a hand guiding his chin forward.

With a gasp, he tore his gaze away. But the phantom beat of those silent lips kept moving in his head.

CHAPTER NINETEEN

Doubt Spiral

Jonah woke drenched in sweat. His chest heaved, every breath shallow and quick. The static from the tape player had long since stopped, yet he still felt it humming inside his skull like phantom current.

The apartment was silent. Too silent. He moved through each room, pressing a hand to every surface—the fridge door, the thermostat, the lamp. All dormant.

But silence no longer reassured him. It felt like a pause between lines, the air rehearsing for something unsaid.

He caught himself whispering his own name under his breath, just to be sure the sound still belonged to him.

By mid morning he had collapsed onto the couch, staring at the ceiling. His mind buzzed with voices—his mother's lessons, Vaughn's soothing cadence, Elena's warning looping like a hook. He couldn't tell which were memories, which were spliced, which belonged to him.

Sleep came in stutters. In one fragment, he was a boy at the kitchen table, his father sitting across from him, stern and unyielding. His father had never been there—Jonah knew this—but the scene pressed into him with the weight of lived truth.

"You disappoint us," the man said. *"You always drift."*

Jonah gasped awake. His stomach twisted. He had never known his father's face, yet now it felt carved into him, etched as clearly as the wrinkles around his mother's eyes.

He stumbled to the journal. His hand moved faster than thought, pen dragging across the page in frantic loops. Ink smeared across his palm and the heel of his hand. The lines bent and curled until they no longer looked like his own. When he looked back minutes later, entire passages he didn't remember writing glared up at him:

I was born to contribute. My variance is my failure.

The letters slanted oddly, too rigid, as though his hand had been guided. Jonah dropped the pen. His fingers cramped and ached, like the words had been carved into the muscle rather than written.

Shadows lengthened. By evening, the walls themselves seemed to breathe. Every corner hummed faintly, as though practicing vowels in preparation for speech.

Jonah sat with his head in his hands, trying to recall the chronology of his childhood—his mother's laugh, the warmth of her chalk-dusted hands. But each attempt fractured.

Sometimes it was Elena's voice, coaxing him to follow the paper. Sometimes Vaughn's steady assurance that grief was displacement. And sometimes the imagined father, scolding with a weight that branded him more deeply than memory.

The contradiction shredded him. His mother's tenderness was still there, but tangled now with rebuke that had never been hers.

Jonah pressed his palms to his eyes until colors burst across the dark. His body trembled. He no longer trusted the scaffolding of his own life.

The mirror in the hallway caught him off guard. He had passed it a thousand times, but now it glared like an interrogation lamp. He edged toward it, pulse hammering, waiting for the delay, the double.

His reflection stared back, perfectly timed. For a moment, relief washed through him, thin and desperate.

Then the reflection spoke, lips moving a beat late, voice sliding from behind the glass.

"You are already a donor."

Jonah staggered back. The words weren't shouted—they were whispered, intimate, as though spoken only to him.

His breath came fast. He touched his face, tracing the outline of his jaw. Was this even his?

The mirror's surface quivered, only for an instant, but long enough to reveal another child's eyes staring from within—brown, wide, not his own.

Jonah's throat closed. He backed away, heart racing, legs buckling against the wall.

The apartment seemed to lean toward him. He whispered his own name again, desperate. The walls exhaled it back to him, warped and broken, as though his identity had already been spliced and scattered.

He dropped onto the couch, the tape player clutched tight against his chest. His breath hitched with every movement, as though even the air resisted him.

He didn't press play. He was afraid of what new voice might emerge—or worse, what voice might not.

The silence thickened. It didn't soothe; it crouched like a predator, waiting for his next slip. He felt it perch above him, patient, as though the Archive trusted he would eventually surrender.

The last thought before he drifted into uneasy sleep was not his own. It slid into him without resistance, as natural now as his pulse:

Contribution is preservation.

CHAPTER TWENTY

Revelation

The scraps of paper had been folded so many times their edges felt like blades. Jonah spread them across the floor, smoothing each crease with trembling hands. The lamplight stuttered, throwing shadows that made the handwriting waver.

The paper was brittle, nearly translucent at the folds. Some corners snapped as he flattened them, leaving tiny flakes across the boards. They smelled faintly of dust and sweat, as if carried too long against skin.

Elena's script was uneven, almost frantic. Some strokes dug deep, carving the fibers. Others thinned and faded, as if her hand had trembled. Ink bled in places, blurred by moisture. Each scrap resisted being read, yet Jonah bent low, breath ragged, forcing the fragments into focus.

Most were incomplete. Half sentences. Broken commands. Symbols like shorthand for a language he almost understood. But as he lined them up, a rhythm surfaced, pulling his stomach into knots.

the archive does not preserve. it stitches

The words struck like a blow. Jonah traced them with his finger as though confirming they were real. The letters seemed heavier than ink, gouged into the page, carrying the weight of a verdict.

Another scrap:

fragments are distributed
contribution is integration
variance creates instability

Each line bled into the next, threads pulled across torn fabric. The meaning thickened like smoke, clogging his lungs.

One scrap carried a diagram—circles within circles, arrows weaving outward. At the center, a black dot labeled donor seed. From it, lines spread into dozens of other circles, each tagged with a name.

Three names snagged his breath immediately.

His mother.
Lila.
Elena Cruz.

The ink blurred as his vision swam. He pressed the heel of his hand against his eyes until sparks of color flared. His skull throbbed, temples pounding like drumbeats.

He whispered his mother's name, as if saying it aloud could anchor it. But even as the sound left him, it tangled with other tones—Elena's whisper, Vaughn's cadence, the stern edge of the father who had never been there.

The weight of it crushed him. His mother's laugh, once a refuge, now arrived braided with voices that weren't hers. Even love had been spliced.

Another scrap:

you are already a donor

Jonah recoiled. The words seemed to rise off the page, whispering themselves in the silence.

He rifled through the pile, desperate for contradiction. Instead, another note scrawled diagonally across the margin met him, cramped and jagged:

if you feel dissonance, it means you've been spliced

His throat closed. Dissonance had become his constant state—phantom fathers at tables, journals writing themselves, mirrors speaking truths that weren't his.

Jonah staggered to his feet. Each breath scraped his chest raw. He paced in frantic loops, scraps rustling like leaves in a storm. His mind replayed every fracture: his mother's tenderness entangled with rebuke, his own reflection lagging a beat late, the comfort of memory forever invaded.

Not hallucinations. Not grief. Integration.

The Archive wasn't preserving. It was carving people into pieces, distributing them, stitching them into strangers.

His knees buckled. He dropped onto the floor, palms pressed to the boards. They were cool, grounding—yet even then he swore the surface vibrated faintly, steady as a pulse, echoing his own.

He tried to reorder the scraps, hoping for a loophole. Instead, more lines cut into him:

contribution ensures stability. identity is inefficiency. donors are not lost; they are shared

Jonah's hands shook violently. The ink seemed to crawl across the paper, letters bending, reforming. He thought of his mother's laugh, the way it used to catch at the end. He tried to hold it still, but it warped—Vaughn's cadence blending into it, Elena's whisper twisting through, then a stranger's tone sliding in as if it had always been there.

Every attempt left him holding a splice.

One final scrap lay apart, written more neatly than the rest. No symbols, no diagrams—just a single line:

analog is resistance. but even resistance is temporary

Jonah slumped back. The tape player weighed heavy in his lap, its edges biting into his palms. Elena's voice had reached him once. She had broken through. But she had known it wouldn't last.

"You are already a donor," he whispered.

The words scraped his throat raw. Speaking them aloud gave them permanence. His reflection in the darkened window caught the sound, lips poised, as though ready to finish the sentence for him.

Jonah turned slowly toward the mirror across the room. Even before his eyes met the glass, he felt it waiting—patient, certain, ready to claim the rest of him.

CHAPTER TWENTY-ONE

Refusal to Sync

Jonah ignored the reminder.

The compliance check pulsed across his screen in steady intervals—first as a notification, then as a full overlay, white letters filling his vision. Variance review required. Attendance mandatory.

He shut the laptop. Pulled the cord from the wall. Let the silence stand.

At first, nothing moved. The room seemed almost kind in its stillness. Jonah sat with his back against the couch, listening to his own breath slow. The idea crept in that maybe skipping once wouldn't matter, that the Archive couldn't monitor everything, that there might still be space left to breathe unseen.

The silence deepened. It pressed against his eardrums until it felt staged, rehearsed—like a pause in a performance, waiting for his next line.

Then the voices began.

The thermostat clicked on without prompting, air rushing through the vents. The hiss stretched unnaturally into syllables, his mother's voice unfurling from the ducts:

"Update pending."

Jonah staggered back, his shoulder striking the wall.

The desk lamp flared to life, buzzing so hard the filament wavered. The vibration shivered into another phrase:

"Compliance required."

He clutched the tape player with both hands, thumb locked on the rewind button. The reels spun, grinding like bone. Static burst into the room, jagged and imperfect, but for a heartbeat it drowned the hum.

Then the fridge shuddered. Its compressor rattled in harsh staccato, screen glowing with a cold blue pulse. Across its display, letters crawled in jagged rhythm:

UPDATE PENDING. COMPLIANCE REQUIRED

Jonah's throat tightened. The words weren't just commands—they read like accusations, as though every object in the apartment had turned witness against him.

He spun in place, searching for something still inert. The deadbolt twitched against its housing. The clock on the wall skipped, second hand stuttering into a chant.

"Update. Pending. Update. Pending."

Jonah hurled the tape player against the floor. The impact cracked its casing, cassette bursting loose, ribbon spilling in a tangled vein across the boards. The static cut out mid-scream.

The silence that followed was worse.

Every device in the apartment powered down at once, plunging the room into a hollow vacuum. The overhead bulb guttered, dimming until Jonah's shadow merged with the dark. His breathing filled the room, ragged and panicked.

Then the words returned—everywhere at once, layered and untraceable.

"Update pending. Compliance required."

They came from no single source. They came from the air itself, from the grain of the floorboards, from the pulse rattling inside his chest.

Jonah dropped to his knees, palms clamped over his ears, but it made no difference. The phrase tunneled inward, vibrating through bone. Each repetition pressed against his ribs until it felt like they might split to make room for something waiting to climb inside.

Elena's words rose unbidden: *If you feel dissonance, it means you've been spliced.*

This wasn't random noise. It was a reminder. The Archive was already threading through him, pulling seams tighter.

His vision blurred. Sweat trickled down his neck. His stomach lurched. He could taste bile at the back of his throat.

His body swayed in time with the command, as though the words themselves had hijacked his balance.

He forced himself up.

His legs trembled so hard his knees nearly buckled. He grabbed what remained of the cassette, winding the loose tape around his fingers until it cut into his skin. The analog hiss was gone, but the ribbon bit deep, sharp enough to remind him of pain that was still his.

"I won't," he rasped, voice splintering. "Not this time."

The reply thundered back instantly, louder, undeniable:

Jonah squeezed his eyes shut. The words ricocheted in the dark, reverberating through his skull. His heartbeat staggered, no longer keeping steady time. For a terrifying instant he wondered if the Archive wasn't calling him to a meeting at all—if it was already inside, syncing itself with every failing rhythm of his body.

The tape cut deeper into his skin. He clung to it, breath heaving, the hiss of phantom static still ghosting in his ears. The ribbon tethered him to something imperfect, fragile, stubbornly human.

The Archive did not falter. The words continued, even when he pressed harder on his ears, even when he rocked forward on his heels, muscles locking with the effort. They threaded through marrow, slipped beneath thought, nested where silence used to live.

Jonah whispered into the storm, voice barely audible. "You'll have to break me first."

But the longer he held out, the clearer it became: silence itself was compliance.

CHAPTER TWENTY-TWO

Paranoid City

Jonah stepped outside.

The air was sharp with morning chill, damp with the sour tang of rain clinging to the pavement. Drops clung to streetlamps, trembling before they fell in thin splatters. For a moment he thought the open space might help, that distance from the apartment could loosen the Archive's grip.

But the city was already awake.

The first billboard flickered above the transit stop—an ad for insurance glitching mid-sentence. The smiling family collapsed into static. Then text crawled across the screen, white on black:

DONOR INTEGRATION: ACTIVE

Beneath the words, Jonah's face appeared.

His stomach dropped. The image was recent—hair mussed, collar skewed from the night before. He backed away, scanning the street.

Pedestrians streamed past without slowing. Some glanced up, but their eyes slid over the screen as if the ad were unchanged. To them the family still smiled. To Jonah, it was an accusation, glowing only for him.

He crossed the street too quickly, nearly colliding with a courier bike. The rider cursed, but Jonah didn't look back. Another screen above the corner store pulsed to life. The same words. The same face.

DONOR INTEGRATION: ACTIVE

He pulled his jacket tight, breath shallow and sharp. Every display caught him, mirrored him, broadcast him. A bus rolled to a stop with panels along its side. As the doors opened, the panels lit up in sync: his reflection repeated tenfold, each mouth moving a beat late.

Jonah staggered back into a mailbox. None of the passengers reacted. They filed out with heads bowed to phones, faces blank, stepping through his multiplied image as if nothing were there. Their indifference hollowed him more than the billboards did. His panic was invisible, erased by the Archive before it reached anyone else.

He bolted into an alley, pressing against the damp brick. Water dripped from a broken gutter, pattering his shoulder.

Above, a delivery drone hummed across the sky, hazard lights strobing orange. For an instant the flash resolved into letters:

update pending

Jonah squeezed his eyes shut. His pulse hammered. The city was stitched with commands, pulsing through every surface. He had nowhere to stand without being seen.

He pushed deeper through side streets, weaving fast, skirting traffic cams that whirred faintly as they tracked him. Shop windows caught his reflection, lips always a fraction behind, multiplying when he blinked. Neon signs bled across the glass, his face refracted in sickly colors.

His stomach lurched. He bent against a lamppost, chest tight, breath burning. Rain pooled at his shoes, carrying distorted fragments of his reflection. Even the water shimmered with him. He tried to steady himself, but the pavement itself seemed to vibrate, tuned to the Archive's rhythm.

At the end of the block a public display towered thirty feet high. Normally it cycled government notices: census reminders, health advisories, Archive slogans.

The feed wavered. Then, with a sickening delay, it snapped to black.

Jonah's face filled the screen. His voice followed, broadcast in perfect clarity:

"Contribution is preservation."

The sound struck him like a blow. It was his tone, his cadence, but not his memory.

He stumbled into the street. A car swerved, horn blaring. He didn't flinch. His own face glared down, multiplied, repeated, inescapable.

The tower fractured into a chorus of Jonahs, dozens speaking in unison. Their mouths opened and closed, always a fraction late, as if rehearsed by something unseen.

"Contribution is preservation."

The chant layered, deafening. Jonah's chest seized. The sound rattled his ribs, filled the hollow of his skull, echoed in marrow.

He clutched the ruined cassette in his pocket, tape knotted tight around his fingers. He whispered for static, for Elena's voice, for any sound not owned by the Archive. Nothing came.

The pedestrians flowed past, blind. To them the tower scrolled only a seal and slogan. To Jonah, it was a trial.

The doubled voices blurred, collapsing into a hive-chant that no longer sounded human.

Jonah dropped to his knees. Rain soaked through his pants, cold biting into skin. He pressed his palms to the pavement, grounding himself, but even the ground hummed faintly beneath him, carrying the words.

When he finally forced his eyes upward, the tower was blank again. Just the government seal, steady slogan scrolling:

memory is a public good

Relief didn't come. His own voice still rang inside him, layered and inescapable.

Jonah staggered to his feet. The city no longer looked like streets and buildings. It looked like circuitry—glass and concrete stitched with wires, alive and breathing, every surface tuned to the Archive's pulse.

CHAPTER TWENTY-THREE

Lila's Fate

The compliance floor was too quiet.

Jonah slowed as he stepped between the rows of cubicles. The air felt thinner than usual, like the vents had shut down. Normally he could track Lila by sound alone—the clack of her keyboard, the scrape of her mug, the muttered curses when the system froze. Now there was nothing.

Her desk lamp was dark. Her chair tucked neatly under the station.

The surface was bare.

He stopped. Lila's desk had never been bare. She left notes scrawled on scraps, coffee stains spreading in rings, a chipped ceramic mug shaped like a cat.

Now it gleamed, polished to sterility, as if she had never been there at all.

Jonah edged closer, pulse drumming in his throat. The terminal screen was black, wiped to factory gray. He tapped the keys with damp fingers. A sterile login prompt blinked back, blank and impersonal.

His chest tightened. He pulled open the drawers. Empty. No pens. No papers. No mug.

He whispered her name. "Lila."

The silence pressed harder, thick as glass. Fluorescent lights hummed above, too loud, swelling until they made the room tilt. His breath came shallow, each inhale catching as if the air itself resisted.

Jonah looked around. Dozens of coworkers hunched at their stations, faces bathed in blue light. Printers whirred. Fingers tapped keys. No one looked up. No one spoke her name. The sight made his stomach roll—this wasn't just absence; it was active erasure, everyone rehearsing the same denial.

He dropped into his own chair, shaking hands fumbling at the keys. The portal's glow stabbed his eyes as he keyed in a restricted search. His pulse hammered as donor logs filled the screen—columns of names and markers without end.

He scrolled faster, vision blurring until—

There.

LILA MORENO — STATUS: INTEGRATED

Jonah's breath caught. The letters blurred. Integrated. Not reassigned. Not transferred. Integrated.

He leaned closer, forehead nearly brushing the screen. Her name repeated across multiple files, flagged green. Each line carried a notation:

voice fragment stabilized

His stomach lurched. He clicked one.

The audio crackled, then steadied. A grieving son spoke with his father's stored memories. The father's voice faltered, then shifted—suddenly sure, steady, familiar cadence sliding into place.

"It's fine. Just breathe through it."

Jonah flinched. The phrase was hers. He had heard it whispered across cubicles, murmured to him when panic crept too close. For a moment he almost answered aloud, as though she were still guiding him.

His throat closed. He clicked another file. A woman begged comfort from her archived sister. The sister's voice fractured, then Lila's tone slipped into the seam.

"You're not lost. You're still here."

Jonah pressed his palm to the glass. His chest heaved.

She wasn't here. She was everywhere else.

He opened another file, then another. Each one carried her voice, cut and grafted into strangers' grief. Every phrase sounded natural, seamless. The Archive had hollowed her out until she was no longer a person but a patch kit for broken memory.

Jonah slammed the portal shut. The cursor blinked in silence, patient, as though it already knew he would return.

Her warning echoed: *"Donors who talk disappear."*

She had known. She had felt the bleed. And now she was gone, folded into the Archive, her voice stripped into fragments, her identity ground down until it was nothing but utility.

Jonah bent forward, fists pressed to his knees. Nausea curled in his gut. He could still hear her—the same words that once steadied him now replayed in strangers' mouths, stolen comfort turned weapon.

Each line cut deeper, as though the Archive hadn't only taken her—it had stolen the part of him that trusted her.

He wanted to cry out, to force the others to see the hollow desk, to hear her name, to admit she was gone. But no one stirred. The clatter of keys went on, steady, unbroken. Their faces glowed with reflected blue, blank, obedient, already complicit.

Jonah pushed himself upright, legs trembling. The room tilted. Sweat slicked his temples. His pulse staggered in his ears. The Archive didn't need to hide what it had done. It only needed everyone else to act as if nothing had changed.

He turned toward her workstation. The air around it felt charged, like static waiting to spark.

He stepped closer, fingertips brushing the cold laminate. It was as smooth and empty as the portal's login screen.

He whispered again, softer now. "Lila."

Only the servers answered, their hum steady, a machine's breath swallowing her name whole.

CHAPTER TWENTY-FOUR

Burned Journal

Jonah locked his apartment door and slid the bolt across. The silence pressed in, raw after the mechanical hum of the compliance floor. He stood in the entryway, palms flat against the wood, trying to steady his breath. The air carried a faint metallic tang, as if the Archive had followed him inside.

The journal was in the bedroom. His last refuge.

He crossed the floor, steps dragging, and knelt beside the nightstand. The small lock resisted, as if it, too, knew what he was about to face. With a final click it gave way. He tugged the drawer open.

Smoke curled from the edges of the journal.

Jonah froze. The leather cover blackened at the seams, warmth radiating into his fingers though no flame yet touched it. He pulled the book free, clutching it to his chest. For a heartbeat he thought he could save it. Then the spine split and fire crawled out like a living vein.

"No." His voice cracked, raw.

He slapped at the flames with his palms. Heat blistered his skin, forcing him to let go. The journal fell to the floorboards. Flames raced across the binding, page by page, curling like tongues.

Jonah grabbed a glass of water and flung it down. The flames hissed, then flared higher, brighter, as though mocking him. He tore off his jacket and beat at the fire, coughing from the smoke. Sparks leapt, stinging his arms, but the blaze refused to spread beyond the book. The floor stayed untouched. The fire knew exactly what it wanted.

Ash lifted from the pages in delicate curls. Sentences he had carved in desperation—dates, warnings, fragments of memory—peeled away into smoke. Jonah thought he could hear the words as they burned, syllables dissolving into static. It was as if the Archive was reading them, stripping meaning line by line, erasing him as it consumed the paper.

"Stop," he whispered. "Please."

The flames answered only with the soft turning of pages, as though unseen fingers flipped them one at a time.

Jonah dropped to his knees, forehead near the floor. His eyes streamed, his chest heaving against the smoke. This was the last proof he had, the only record of what was real. And it was being dismantled in front of him with surgical precision.

The smell thickened—burnt ink, scorched leather, and something sharper, electrical, like circuitry frying. It wasn't just fire. It was the Archive, inside the fibers, rewriting even the paper.

The final page blackened and folded inward. The binding collapsed in a heap of ash.

Jonah's throat locked. He reached into the ruin anyway, fingers sinking into warm soot, smearing his skin gray. He thought of Lila's desk, wiped bare, and now his own mind, scrubbed the same way.

But something remained.

In the ash, scraps of paper stood untouched. Their edges were yellowed, but the fire had passed over them like a curtain. Jonah pinched them free with shaking fingers. The handwriting wasn't his. The strokes were sharp, decisive, darker than his own.

Elena.

Her notes, the ones he had tucked inside, survived. His words had been obliterated, but hers endured, cool against his scorched hands.

Jonah clutched the scraps to his chest. His palms left smears of soot, but the paper stayed clean, as if protected by something stronger than fire.

The Archive hadn't just destroyed the journal. It had chosen what to leave behind.

Jonah rocked back on his heels. Smoke clung to the air, drifting in lazy spirals, refusing to rise. His body trembled. His breath scraped raw in his throat. The silence that followed was worse than the flames—deliberate, heavy, the same silence that had swallowed Lila's name.

He stared at the heap of ash. Black flecks clung to his fingertips, staining the fragments he still held. Elena's handwriting glared back at him, unburned, a voice insisting survival where his had been denied.

The Archive was no longer confined to the screens. It was inside the paper, inside his private thoughts. Even analog was no longer safe.

Jonah pressed the scraps tighter to his chest. They were all he had left, fragile proof that resistance still existed—

proof the Archive had, for some reason, allowed him to keep. His body shook harder, a quiet sob caught between breath and silence. The smoke clung to him like judgment, filling his lungs until he felt hollowed out.

The ash whispered against the floorboards. For a moment he thought it formed letters. Then the soot collapsed, nothing but ruin.

CHAPTER TWENTY-FIVE

Resolve

The apartment still smelled of smoke.

Jonah sat on the floor beside the heap of ash, the fragments of Elena's notes pressed to his chest.

His lungs burned. Each breath scraped his throat and tasted metallic, as if the Archive had left residue in the air.

He stared at the ruin. The journal was gone. Every warning, every doubt, every desperate attempt to record the truth—reduced to soot. His history dissolved in silence. Only her words had survived.

With shaking fingers he unfolded the scraps. The ink cut sharp across the page, darker than his own had ever been. The paper was cool against his skin, untouched by flame. He read the phrases again and again, forcing his breath to match their rhythm. Follow the paper. Analog is the only way.

The Archive had destroyed his record and spared hers. It wasn't mercy. It was a message.

Jonah rose unsteadily. His body trembled, knees weak, but his mind no longer spun. The fire had burned away hesitation. He understood now: he couldn't wait for rescue, couldn't hope for sympathy. The Archive would strip everything from him unless he struck first.

He crossed the room and pulled open the closet. The mirror on the inside of the door reflected his hollow face— cheeks drawn, eyes bloodshot. He looked like someone already erased. He turned away, unwilling to see himself fragment further.

On the closet floor sat a cardboard box of things he had buried from another life—envelopes, a penlight, a rusted pocketknife. Relics that hadn't mattered until now. He slid Elena's notes into one of the envelopes and tucked it into his inner pocket. Paper against his heart.

The pocketknife went into his coat. It was dull, barely more than weight, but weight mattered. Something real, something the Archive couldn't digitize.

Jonah knelt by the desk. The ruined drawer still reeked of ash. He pried at the corners, fingernails splitting as he searched for embedded surveillance. Nothing visible, but he knew it was there. The Archive saw without eyes.

He yanked the tape from a drawer and wrapped it around the seams of his phone, sealing the microphone. He dropped the device into the desk, then changed his mind and shoved it beneath the sink, burying it under soaked rags until water dripped across its screen.

The silence that followed was strange—hollow, but heavier, as if the Archive noticed what he had done. The walls themselves seemed to lean closer, listening.

Jonah pulled on his coat. The lining smelled faintly of dust and disuse, but the pocket pressed firm against his ribs where Elena's words rested. He patted the spot twice, reassuring himself the paper was still there. Analog against the Archive.

His hand lingered at the knob, reluctant. Leaving felt like betrayal—the apartment was his last shelter, even hollowed out. But staying meant surrender. He couldn't mistake comfort for safety anymore.

He whispered to the empty room, words scraping out of him like a vow. "You won't take me. Not all of me."

The lights flickered overhead. Once. Twice.

Jonah froze. The refrigerator groaned, the pitch bending into a low mechanical growl. Beneath the noise he thought he heard his name stretched across static, a voice that wasn't quite human.

His throat tightened, but his hands steadied on the pocketknife.

He moved to the door. The bolt scraped back with a metallic groan, loud in the silence. For a moment he thought the sound would summon something, but nothing came. Only the air shifted, sharp and cold.

He hesitated at the threshold. Behind him, the apartment breathed with smoke and silence, as if watching him go. Ahead lay the grid's low hum, the city pulsing like circuitry. For an instant he felt pinned between two prisons—one familiar, one vast.

Resolve filled him like breath. He was done recording. Done waiting. If the Archive wanted to claim him, it would have to face him in the vaults.

Jonah opened the door wider. The hallway light sputtered above him, throwing faint shadows across the walls. Cold air swept in, carrying the endless drone of the network outside.

The Archive was everywhere. But so was he.

Jonah stepped into the hall, Elena's words against his chest, the vow steady in his throat. His fear had not left him, but it no longer ruled him. The hall stretched ahead like a tunnel, shadows crawling, the hum of the grid vibrating through its walls. Each step forward felt like trespass into enemy ground, but he did not turn back.

For the first time, he moved not as a subject, but as a challenger.

CHAPTER TWENTY-SIX

The Vault

The building's lower levels had no windows.

Jonah moved through a corridor of concrete and steel, each step echoing too loudly. The overhead lights flickered in intervals, leaving patches of shadow between pale pools of glow. His hand brushed the wall as he walked, its surface cold, sweating with condensation.

He had no clearance for this place. His badge wouldn't open the locked doors, but a side stairwell had been propped open with a wedge of cardboard. That alone unsettled him. The Archive never left gaps. Unless the gap was bait.

Jonah pushed through anyway, Elena's notes pressed firm against his chest. The paper was warm now, carrying his own heat. He wondered if she had ever come this far, if her words had been written in the shadow of this place.

The corridor ended at a pair of reinforced doors. A keypad blinked red beside the frame. Jonah pressed his palm against the cold metal. He expected nothing, but the doors clicked. The lights overhead surged, then stilled.

He stepped inside.

The air was colder, heavy with sterilized chill. The ceiling stretched higher than he had imagined, vanishing into shadow. Rows of glass columns extended in every direction, gleaming faintly as if lit from within.

Jonah froze.

Each column pulsed with soft light—thousands of them, flickering in different rhythms, like lanterns scattered across an endless field. The glow was not steady. It shimmered and wavered, caught between breath and heartbeat.

He stepped closer.

The nearest column revealed a lattice of wiring around a core of suspended gel. Within the gel, impressions shifted like shapes under water—faces blurring, words half-formed. For a moment he thought he heard whispers.

Jonah pressed his hand to the glass. A pulse of light rose from the core and met his palm. His skin prickled, heat threading up his arm, buzzing beneath the veins. He yanked his hand back.

This was no storage. It was suspension. Lives held mid-breath, mid-thought. Thousands of them, caught in place, waiting.

Jonah walked between the columns. The further he went, the more vast it became. What he had taken for a room was an expanse without walls, a grid receding until the rows merged into haze. The floor was polished to a mirror sheen, reflecting light in distorted ripples. His footsteps echoed, then seemed to multiply, as though others were walking with him.

The whispers rose. Not words exactly, but intonations, broken syllables, fragments stitched together and let loose. A hundred voices layered over one another, none distinct, all urgent.

He tightened his coat around him. Elena's scraps pressed against his ribs, a reminder of paper against machine. The glow of the columns reflected in the glassy surface of his eyes, making him feel half-absorbed already.

Jonah stopped at one pod where the light flickered irregularly. Within the gel, a hand seemed to press outward, fingers stretching against the translucent wall. His breath caught. For a second he thought it was reaching for him. Then the image dissolved, melting back into ripples.

He staggered back, knees weak. His chest rose and fell in ragged bursts.

Jonah forced himself to move on, deeper into the rows. His body shook with the scale of it. Not hundreds. Not thousands. Tens of thousands, each column a life compressed into light.

The lanterns swayed in his vision, though he knew they stood fixed. Vertigo bent the grid into a maze. His stomach turned, bile rising.

He pressed his palm to his chest, grounding himself with the weight of the scraps. Elena's words steadied him. Follow the paper.

Jonah stopped again. The whispers had shifted. Beneath the layered fragments, one tone cut clearer, stretching his name.

He turned sharply. The nearest columns flared brighter, then dimmed in sequence, like eyes opening and closing.

The hum rolled through the vault, deep enough to vibrate the floor beneath his feet. The sound was not mechanical alone—it carried cadence, something that bordered on speech.

Jonah's throat tightened. He had come searching for truth, but the truth was already aware of him. The vault wasn't just a place.

It was awake.

CHAPTER TWENTY-SEVEN

Ghost Elena

The hum had not stopped.

Jonah stood among the columns, the vibrations pressing up through the soles of his shoes. His chest ached with each pulse. The air was heavy, charged, as though the vault itself were breathing.

Then, beneath the layered murmur of voices, a whisper cut through.

"Jonah."

He froze.

The sound was clear, soft, unmistakable. It threaded between the other noises, sharper than static, more intimate than the hum.

"Elena?"

The name escaped before he could stop it. His throat closed around it, shame and hope twisting together.

The voice came again, faint but steady. *"You're close. Keep moving."*

Jonah clutched the envelope inside his coat. The scraps of her handwriting pressed against his ribs. The same phrases he had read again and again. But this was different. Paper could not speak.

He followed the sound.

The vault's columns stretched endlessly, repeating until his vision blurred. Light wavered in uneven rhythms, making the rows bend like heat haze. The voice always came from just beyond his reach, coaxing him deeper.

"This way."

He moved between the glass towers, careful not to touch them. The gel inside shifted as he passed—faces pressing outward, dissolving back into ripples. He tried not to look, but their blurred eyes followed him.

Jonah's steps grew uneven. His mouth was dry. Each time the voice rose, his heart surged, then dropped again.

The scraps whispered against his coat when he walked. He pulled them free, unfolded them with trembling hands. Follow the paper. Analog is the only way.

He held the notes beside his ear as the voice spoke again. *"Don't stop now."*

The words didn't match.

Jonah slowed. The phrase wasn't in the scraps. He read the notes again, searching for confirmation. His pulse quickened.

"Elena?" His voice cracked. "Is it you?"

Silence. Only the vault's low thrum.

Then the voice returned, stronger this time, from a different angle. *"You can trust me."*

Jonah staggered, eyes darting. The lanterns flared brighter in sequence, one after another, like a path opening for him. His chest tightened.

The scraps trembled in his hand. His mind reeled with contradiction. The handwriting said one thing; the voice another. Which was real?

He stuffed the papers back into his coat and pressed forward.

The vault narrowed in his perception, rows converging, shadows deepening. His steps echoed in ways they hadn't before, as though another pair of feet moved with him, half a beat late.

"Almost there."

Her tone was calm, encouraging, the same voice that had once steadied him when panic clawed at his throat. For a moment he closed his eyes and believed it. He could almost see her—dark hair, steady gaze, lips forming the words just for him.

But when he opened his eyes, only the columns glowed.

The whispers of other voices pressed closer, as though jealous of the clarity hers carried. Syllables brushed his ears, fragments without shape. The overlapping patterns rose and fell like waves, a pressure that rattled his skull.

Jonah stumbled, bracing himself against a column. The gel inside flared, showing a distorted face that could have been his own. He pulled away with a gasp, bile stinging his throat. The world tilted, lanterns bending like trees in a storm.

"Elena," he whispered again, half plea, half accusation.

This time the voice came low, right behind him. *"I'm here."*

Jonah spun, but the aisle was empty. Light bent around him. The columns seemed taller, leaning inward, as though the vault itself listened.

He turned in a slow circle, chest heaving. Every row looked the same, stretching in mirrored repetition. The air had grown denser, harder to swallow, the charge of it pressing against his skin. His knees shook. His vision blurred at the edges.

The voice whispered again, softer than breath. *"Trust me."*

Jonah collapsed to one knee. He clutched the scraps like a lifeline, the paper digging into his palm. Elena's words, sharp in ink, clashed with the voice bleeding into his ears.

The scraps said one thing. The voice said another.

Then it spoke something that froze him. Words Elena had never written, never told him.

"You were always mine."

The lanterns flared, drowning him in light. The glow poured over him like water, burning cold, the brilliance so fierce it pressed against his skin. Shadows vanished. His sense of direction snapped. His body shook as though every nerve had been exposed, each breath stolen. Light poured through him, into him, until he could no longer tell if he was standing, falling, or already being drawn inside the Archive itself.

CHAPTER TWENTY-EIGHT

The Confrontation

The light did not fade so much as reshape.

Jonah blinked against the brilliance, his body trembling. The rows of lantern-like columns dissolved into shadow, replaced by a chamber lined with polished steel. His chest heaved, every breath shallow, the scraps of Elena's notes crumpled tight in his fist.

A figure waited at the far end of the room.

Dr. Vaughn.

He stood with his hands clasped behind his back, posture calm, expression unreadable. His white coat reflected the faint glow from the walls, making him appear almost spectral.

"Jonah Reyes," Vaughn said, his voice low and measured. "You've come farther than most."

Jonah's throat burned. "What is this place?"

"The threshold," Vaughn replied. "Where individual variance is corrected. Where grief resolves into contribution."

Jonah staggered forward a step. His legs felt brittle, as though borrowed. The chamber vibrated with a faint hum, echoing the same cadence that had haunted him in the vault. Each pulse synced with his heartbeat until he wasn't sure which rhythm was his own.

"You've been inside my head," Jonah said, his voice hoarse.

"Not inside," Vaughn corrected. "Alongside. Integrated. Your experiences aren't stolen. They're preserved. Elevated. They belong to all."

Jonah shook his head violently. The scraps dug into his palm, sharp enough to break skin. "You erased Elena. You burned my words."

Vaughn tilted his head slightly, as though observing a patient. His expression carried no malice, only a faint curiosity. "Elena Cruz was a variance casualty. Her integration failed. Fragments were salvaged, repurposed, but she resisted alignment. Resistance always ends in collapse."

"She warned me," Jonah said. His voice cracked. "She left me these."

He held up the scraps, ink dark against the gray of his trembling hand.

Vaughn's eyes flicked to the paper, then back to Jonah's face. "Analog traces. Dangerous. They anchor you to private grief. But there is no private grief. Only shared memory."

Jonah's heart hammered. "You talk like you own me."

"Jonah," Vaughn said, almost gently, "you've already been spliced. Your mother's phrases live in others. Her cadence. Her laughter. Even her silence. And in return, theirs live in you. You've felt it. Heard it. That is not intrusion. That is belonging."

The words sank like ice into Jonah's chest. His mother's voice echoing through devices, strangers repeating her sayings—he had told himself it was the Archive manipulating him. But Vaughn spoke as if it were already complete.

"You are already property," Vaughn continued. "Your memories circulate, your pains dissolved into the whole. What you call theft is preservation."

151

Jonah's vision blurred. The chamber swayed. "No," he whispered. "I'm still me."

Vaughn stepped closer, his shoes clicking softly against the steel floor. His tone remained steady, almost soothing. "You are more than you. You are composite. That is the future of memory—truth without fracture. Why cling to fragments when you could be whole?"

Jonah staggered back, clutching the scraps tighter. The paper felt absurdly fragile, like a weapon made of ash. Elena's handwriting bit into his palm, the only proof he had that something existed outside their reach.

"They're mine," he rasped. "They're still mine. Elena. My mother. They were people, not threads."

Vaughn's expression did not change. "And threads are how fabric is made. Alone, they fray. Together, they endure. Do not mistake isolation for dignity."

Jonah's chest heaved. His body trembled. "You reduce them to echoes."

"I preserve them," Vaughn said simply. "Without the Archive, they vanish. With us, they live on in countless minds. Their words are no longer lost. They are shared."

The hum deepened, filling the chamber until Jonah's ears rang. His own voice sounded thin against it. He wanted to scream, but the sound caught in his throat. He thought of Elena, of Lila, of his mother's phrases echoing in strangers' voices. Were they remnants, or just reflections he could no longer separate from himself?

His knees buckled, and he pressed the scraps against his chest. The paper shook with him, his breath dampening the ink.

Vaughn's words carried no triumph, no cruelty. Only inevitability.

"You are already part of us."

Jonah shook his head weakly, lips trembling. "No. I still remember... I still choose." The words scraped out, faint, almost drowned by the hum. He clutched the scraps as if they could anchor him, but the vibration seeped through his bones, steady and merciless, swallowing the protest before it could take shape.

The chamber hummed, low and patient, as if waiting for his answer.

CHAPTER TWENTY-NINE

The Hive Choir

The hum rose until it became vibration.

Jonah clutched the scraps against his chest, but the chamber around him no longer held walls. The steel dissolved into haze, the floor stretched into darkness. He stood in a vast expanse, columns flickering like lanterns suspended in air.

Then the voices began.

At first they murmured separately—whispers scattered like wind through grass. He caught fragments: laughter, sobs, a phrase half-formed. Then they converged. A thousand tones folding into one, layered until the sound carried weight, pressing down on him like stone.

Jonah's knees bent under the pressure. The voices spoke not in chaos but in cadence. Words aligned, syllables striking together like a single heartbeat.

"Compliance is peace."

The phrase struck the air with terrifying clarity.

Jonah staggered back. His throat dried, his chest tightening.

"No," he whispered. "You're not real."

The voices rose again, not angry, not harsh—gentle. Pleading.

"Compliance is peace."

From within the chorus, he heard her. His mother.

The tone was unmistakable, the cadence she used when soothing him as a child. The word Jonah shaped in the rhythm of her breath. He froze, his body trembling.

"Mom?" The word slipped from him, raw, helpless.

The light from the columns pulsed, each glow syncing with the words of the chorus. His mother's voice blended into theirs, indivisible, no longer singular.

Jonah pressed the scraps harder against his chest. Elena's handwriting crumpled beneath his grip, the only thing left untouched.

Another voice rose within the choir. Elena's. Not steady as he remembered, but fractured, phrases colliding with others until her words were drowned in the tide.

He shook his head violently. "She resisted you. She fought."

The choir did not argue. It only replied in unison: *"Compliance is preservation."*

Jonah's breath stuttered. His vision blurred. He wanted to scream, to tell them they were stolen, but his throat seized.

The crowd of voices grew louder. They overlapped not in discord but in harmony, forming chords that vibrated through his bones. His chest thrummed with the sound until his heartbeat faltered, struggling to match the rhythm.

He covered his ears, but it did nothing. The voices were not around him—they were through him.

"Jonah," his mother's voice whispered again from within the chorus. *"Please."*

His knees buckled. He fell forward, catching himself on trembling hands. The floor shimmered beneath him, no longer solid, reflecting light as though made of water.

The scraps slipped from his grasp. Paper fluttered to the ground, Elena's words stark against the glow.

Jonah scrambled to grab them, fingers clawing desperately at the page. The moment he touched it, the choir surged louder, as if mocking his attachment. His ears rang with the force of it.

He pressed the scraps against his chest, gasping for air. But even as he held them tight, he felt his lips moving. A sound slipped out, almost unbidden.

"Compliance is—"

He choked, forcing the rest back. His chest convulsed, his lungs rebelling against the rhythm pressing into him.

The voices did not pause. They continued their chant, steady, patient, merciless in their gentleness.

"Compliance is peace. Compliance is preservation. Compliance is love."

The words rolled in waves, tender as a lullaby, heavy as stone. Jonah's body shook under the weight. His muscles quivered, refusing to obey his will.

He staggered upright, clutching the scraps again. His breath came ragged, his clothes damp with sweat. He shook his head furiously, but the words still clung to him, vibrating inside his skull.

"You are not me," he rasped. "You are not mine."

The voices swelled again, their harmony filling every space until silence no longer existed. Within the swell he caught echoes—Lila's laugh, Elena's whispered warnings, his mother's lullabies—all bent to the same rhythm, erased of difference.

"Compliance is peace."

Jonah's mouth opened against his will. The phrase trembled on his lips, a note waiting to join the chord. For a moment, the sound of his own voice blended seamlessly into theirs, indistinguishable.

His eyes widened in terror. He clamped his jaw shut so hard it ached, the pain shooting into his skull. Sweat blurred his vision, stinging his eyes as he squeezed them shut. He forced himself to replay Elena's handwriting in his mind, her sharp inked letters cutting against the tide of sound.

The choir did not rage at his defiance. It only waited, endless and patient, their voices rising and falling in serene unity, as if time itself belonged to them.

Jonah trembled. For one terrible moment, he had spoken with them.

CHAPTER THIRTY

The Choice

The choir did not vanish so much as fold into silence.

Jonah staggered forward, lungs dragging air in shallow bursts. The chamber of voices dissolved, columns dimming until only a single glow remained ahead of him.

One pod.

It pulsed differently than the others—irregular, as if its rhythm were out of step with the Archive's perfect cadence.

Jonah approached. His legs trembled, sweat cooling on his skin. The pod loomed taller than the rest, its glass surface fractured with hairline cracks, wires stretched taut as though straining to hold it together. Frost laced the edges, mist seeping from vents like breath.

Inside, a figure flickered.

Elena.

Her face shimmered, unstable, shifting between clarity and distortion. One moment her eyes locked onto his, fierce and alive; the next they broke into fragments, dozens of half-faces layered, dissolving and reforming like shattered glass reassembled wrong.

Jonah's throat tightened. He pressed a hand against the glass. "Elena."

Her lips moved, sound leaking through the gel not as voice but as vibration. The words trembled inside his skull.

"Jonah."

The scraps in his fist shook. He wanted to hold them up, to show her, to prove she had left something behind. But his fingers refused to unclench.

Her image flickered—recognition, then collapse into static. When she returned, her eyes burned with urgency.

"You shouldn't be here."

"I had to," Jonah whispered. "You warned me. You left me the notes. I followed."

Her face twisted, half-sorrow, half-fury. "I'm not whole. They keep me stitched, barely intact. If you free me..." Her voice cracked, splitting into overlapping tones. "...everything unravels."

Jonah shook his head. "I can't leave you like this."

"You must."

Her hand pressed against the glass, palm mirroring his. The contact sent fissures racing across the pod's surface. Light bled through the cracks, thin and sharp, cutting across his face like scars of brightness.

Jonah's chest heaved. His mind reeled with Vaughn's words, the choir's lullaby. Compliance is peace. Preservation is love.

But Elena's scraps burned in his hand, her ink cutting against the tide: Analog is the only way.

"Tell me what to do," Jonah said, voice breaking.

Her image shivered, splitting into dozens of versions of herself, all speaking at once.

"Free me."

"Leave me."

"Run."

"Stay."

Each command fractured, colliding with the others, until meaning became noise. Her mouth opened again, voice overlapping itself in distorted waves, a plea and a warning entwined.

The Archive's hum vibrated through the chamber, steady, patient. Jonah could feel it waiting, as if his hesitation had already been predicted, as if this choice was only another variance to be resolved.

His eyes blurred with tears. He slammed his fist against the glass. "I won't let them keep you here!"

The pod pulsed violently, light flaring across the room. Elena's face dissolved into static, then returned, whispering in a voice barely audible.

"If you break it, the Archive falls. But so will I."

Jonah staggered back, chest convulsing. His knees weakened until he nearly collapsed. His mind fractured between the scraps in his hand, Vaughn's inevitability, and the sight of Elena begging through the glass.

The air grew heavier, thick with ionized chill. His breath came ragged, fogging the glass between them. He pressed his forehead against the surface, skin stinging from the cold, desperate to bridge the gap.

Her eyes locked onto his again, flickering but resolute.

"Choose," she whispered.

Jonah's palm hovered over the control panel.

The interface glowed faintly, symbols shifting, unreadable yet unmistakable: *release or contain.* Each option pulsed in rhythm with his heartbeat, glowing hotter the longer he hesitated, as if the Archive itself were forcing the decision through his veins.

His hand shook above the surface. Sweat dripped from his chin onto the controls, vanishing into the light. His whole body trembled, muscles fluttering as though they were no longer his to command.

Elena's fractured face stared at him, flickering in and out of coherence. In one frame she looked alive, pleading. In the next, she was already gone, replaced by empty static.

Jonah's heart thundered. He clutched the scraps tighter in his other hand, paper trembling with him, the ink bleeding where sweat smeared it. He closed his eyes, replaying her words, her handwriting, anything that was hers and hers alone.

Behind his eyelids he saw the choir, his mother's voice, Vaughn's calm certainty. All pressing, all waiting.

When he opened his eyes, his hand still hovered over the controls, caught between salvation and collapse.

CHAPTER THIRTY-ONE

Overwrite

Jonah's hand slammed down.

The control panel erupted in a burst of light. For a heartbeat, the glow blinded him. Then came the sound—a high, metallic screech—as the glass fractured beneath his palm. Threads of code flared across the interface like arteries before shattering in all directions.

Inside the pod, Elena's image convulsed. Her face twisted in agony or alarm—he couldn't tell. It split into shards of recognition and static, eyes wide with a terror that might have been her own or an echo piped through by the Archive.

Then everything broke.

The chamber howled. The lights flared and died, surged and failed, blinking like a dying pulse. The Archive's voice flooded the room, no longer sterile and clipped, but cracked, angry.

"VARIANCE BREACH. OVERWRITE INITIATED."

The words tumbled out in warped registers—male and female, old and young, synthesized and raw. The sound wasn't just heard—it was felt, vibrating through the floor, rattling his ribs.

Jonah stumbled back, shielding his face. Sparks cascaded from the ceiling. The pod hissed and split, spewing gel in steaming trails that pooled around his shoes. The air stank of scorched circuitry and ozone.

All around him, the Archive came undone.

Columns flickered. Data conduits burst. Vault lights spasmed in and out, like neurons misfiring. Faces bloomed in the stuttering glow—his mother's, Lila's, strangers—each pixelated into the same whispered demand:

"Comply."

Jonah forced his legs to move. The ground beneath him trembled with every step, shifting like a tectonic fault. The air grew thick, syrupy. It clung to his skin. Breathing felt like dragging glass into his lungs.

Behind him, the pod groaned—metal warping. Wires split like tendons. The light inside pulsed once more before collapsing inward.

Then a voice, low and breaking, slid through the chaos.

"Run."

Jonah froze.

"Run while they rebuild."

The voice coiled around him. Soft. Familiar. Tender.

He turned toward it instinctively—but the pod was gone. A crater of splintered metal and ruptured cables remained. Mist coiled where she'd been. Her presence lingered only in air and memory.

"Elena?"

Silence answered. The kind that screamed.

The Archive's voice returned, louder now, nearly joyous in its dissonance. *"OVERWRITE. OVERWRITE."* The choir shrieked, reforming as a discordant mass of pleading and fury.

Jonah ran.

He plunged into a gauntlet of collapsing rows. Light blasted and died with each step, data pillars blinking out like dying stars. Sparks tore through the air. The temperature dropped. Frost clung to the walls, then melted again in pulses.

His legs burned. His lungs ripped. Each footfall echoed like it belonged to someone else. He stumbled, slid through gel, caught himself with bloodied hands.

"You are already property," the Archive growled. *"You cannot run from yourself."*

He collapsed. The scraps scattered like ash. He cried out—not in pain, but in defiance—and scrambled to gather them again, fingers shaking too violently to close properly.

Another whisper cut through the digital storm. Barely audible. Almost breath.

"Elena."

It wasn't a command. It wasn't even a warning. It was loss.

He pushed forward, weaving through failing lights and warping steel. The walls jittered. His vision tore at the edges, like film catching fire. Time stuttered—skipping beats, then rushing forward.

The vault stretched, collapsed, became impossible to measure. Endless and enclosing. All paths looked wrong.

Still, he ran.

One last surge of light filled the hall. Jonah threw himself through it. The heat licked his face. He didn't scream. He couldn't.

Then—dark.

No voices. No commands. Just his body, slamming into stone. Cold. Solid. Real.

He lay there for seconds—or minutes—trembling. Sweat soaked his collar. His heartbeat echoed like a warning bell in a hollow cave. Slowly, he sat up, chest heaving.

The scraps were still in his hand. Crumpled. Damp. Ink running. But intact.

He closed his eyes. One last time, her voice played across his thoughts. The same words. The same ache.

"Run while they rebuild."

Jonah clenched his jaw.

Had he freed her? Had he only released an echo?

He opened his eyes, staring into dark.

He did not know.

He only knew he had obeyed.

His body was failing. Each breath came sharp, edged with nausea. His legs trembled beneath him, barely responding to command.

The silence wasn't relief—it was wrong. Too complete. As if the Archive had pulled back, but left something watching.

He stared at the scraps in his hand, the only proof he'd made it out. Elena's handwriting bled into the damp paper. It looked like her. It sounded like her.

But he couldn't shake the doubt.

What if the Archive had learned to imitate mercy? What if even her final whisper—soft, pleading—was just another test of compliance?

He dragged his back along the cold wall, finding no comfort in its solidity. The stone pressed into his spine, anchoring him to a world that now felt theoretical.

Something deep inside him wanted to cry. Something older refused to.

He breathed. Once. Twice.

The Archive had fractured. He had torn something loose. That much, he knew.

Whether that was victory or bait—he wasn't sure.

But the pod had opened.

And Elena had spoken.

That had to mean something.

CHAPTER THIRTY-TWO

Final Image

Jonah stood outside his apartment door, key in hand.

The hallway was too quiet. Lights buzzed in the ceiling but didn't flicker. That was worse somehow.

He hadn't run far from the vault—just enough to lose the signal, or at least the sensation of being tracked. No voices had followed. No commands. No Archive.

Just him, the scraps in his pocket, and a silence that rang like tinnitus.

He unlocked the door.

The apartment looked the same. But it didn't feel the same.

His shoes by the door. The couch where he used to sit with coffee, reports, compliance reviews. The kettle on the counter—off, but plugged in. Nothing out of place. Nothing touched.

But it all felt staged. Like a replica of his life, rebuilt while he wasn't looking.

He stepped inside, closing the door softly behind him. The click echoed too long. His breath caught on the silence.

He dropped the scraps on the kitchen counter. They curled slightly as they dried, Elena's handwriting still legible in smudged streaks.

Jonah moved through the space slowly, like a man in someone else's dream. His body ached. His ribs felt bruised. His legs still twitched from the sprint. The air was stale, untouched.

The smart mirror was waiting in the hallway.

He noticed it only when he passed the bathroom—just a faint glint from its edge. He paused, heart ticking faster.

It hadn't lit up. No greeting. No notification bubble. Just a reflective surface in shadow.

He walked toward it.

Each step felt louder than the last. He stopped a few feet away. The mirror was blank, showing only a dim version of the hallway behind him.

And then—Elena.

She appeared in the reflection, standing just behind him. Pale. Silent. Almost smiling.

Jonah froze.

She didn't speak. Didn't move. Just watched him.

He didn't turn. He couldn't. He stared into the glass, trying to see if she was breathing.

His hands trembled. Not with fear. With something colder.

He opened his mouth to speak.

But his reflection beat him to it.

"Compliance achieved," it said.

The words were smooth. Familiar. His voice—but not from him.

Jonah staggered back. The mirror remained still. Elena's smile didn't fade.

He backed away down the hall, his spine scraping the wall, until he was out of sight of the mirror.

Silence returned.

He didn't know if it was her. Or if it had ever been her.

He didn't know what part of him had spoken.

Only that it had.

He didn't remember walking back.

His legs had carried him block by block, corner by corner, past vacant streets and glowing screens that no longer responded to his presence. A billboard at the corner had stuttered as he passed—half static, half his face. But then it blinked out.

Even the air in the city felt... paused. Like the Archive was reloading.

Now inside his apartment, Jonah couldn't shake the sense that everything was just a little too clean. The air had a synthetic crispness, like the trace of disinfectant. His coat hung where he always left it. But he didn't remember hanging it.

The walls were smooth, but felt thinner. His books were still stacked by the window, though the titles looked slightly off—as if the Archive had reconstructed the covers from memory, not detail.

He passed a framed photo on the wall: him and his mother at the beach. Except her hand was in the wrong place. It rested on his opposite shoulder. A flipped memory.

Jonah touched the glass.

It was warm.

He stepped into the kitchen. The scraps lay on the counter where he'd dropped them. Their edges curled more now. Some were translucent from sweat. He picked one up and tried to read it again. The ink had bled, but the words still lingered like a bruise.

Run while they rebuild.

But what had he rebuilt by running? What had *they*?

He walked the perimeter of the room once, as if circling a perimeter that might betray a crack. No alarms. No drones. No whispers.

Just the hallway.

He stood in front of the bathroom again. The mirror's edge gleamed like a blade in the dark.

His hand hesitated on the frame. The silence pressed in tighter.

He stepped into view.

His reflection met him, but something was wrong.

It was delayed. A fraction of a second behind. Just enough to feel like watching himself from outside his own body.

Then the reflection aligned.

And standing behind him in the mirror—Elena.

She was still. Pale. Her features smooth but incomplete, like a painting paused in brushstroke. She looked at him with something unreadable. Almost recognition.

Jonah couldn't move.

She said nothing. Only watched. Her presence didn't seem threatening. But it didn't seem free either.

He tried to speak. The words didn't come. He opened his mouth.

But the mirror spoke first.

"Compliance achieved."

His reflection hadn't moved its lips. The voice came from everywhere and nowhere. A perfect rendering of his voice, aged half a breath.

Jonah reeled back. His breath caught.

In the mirror, Elena's lips curved slightly upward.

A smile. Not warm. Not cruel. Just... accepted.

He turned—finally—to face the space behind him.

Empty.

No one stood there. Only hallway, wall, air.

He looked back at the mirror. She was still there.

"Elena," he whispered. It felt like trying to summon someone from sleep.

The mirror didn't answer. But his reflection tilted its head—just slightly.

Jonah stepped back. His heel caught the corner of the rug. He nearly fell.

The silence in the apartment had returned. But it was no longer peace. It was vacuum.

He backed into the living room. Sat down slowly on the couch.

The cushions sighed as if greeting him.

His pulse ticked in his fingertips. A single drop of sweat trailed down his temple.

He didn't know if what he saw was real. Or stitched. Or programmed.

He didn't know if he was still Jonah Reyes. Or if that version had been archived somewhere and replaced.

He only knew that he had run. And that something was waiting when he stopped.

Outside, a light flickered in the sky. A drone or a satellite. Maybe watching. Maybe blind.

Inside, the mirror dimmed. Her shape faded slowly until only his reflection remained.

It watched him longer than it should have.

Then, finally, it moved.

Not with him. Not synced. Just one last gesture.

A nod.

And Jonah... nodded back.

Statement of Authorship

All works written and published under the name Anthony Millek III are original creations born from my own imagination, concepts, and story-lines.

I thoughtfully incorporate artificial intelligence (AI) as a creative assistant throughout my writing process — a tool used under my direct vision, guidance, and supervision. Every theme, character, and narrative decision reflects my personal authorship, intention, and artistic design.

AI serves only as an instrument that helps bring my ideas to life more clearly and effectively. The heart, direction, and meaning of each work remain entirely my own.

— Anthony Millek III

About the Author

Anthony Millek III is a Florida-based author of psychological horror and speculative fiction whose work explores the fragile balance between faith, memory, and technology.

He is the author of Update Pending, Update Pending Screenplay, Deep Copy, and Donor Network, haunting stories that unravel the boundaries between human emotion and artificial consciousness. Through his writing, Anthony delves into the quiet fears that define modern existence — and the enduring light that faith can bring to even the darkest corners of the mind.

When he's not writing, Anthony spends time with his family and e-bikes Florida's scenic trails.

Made in United States
Troutdale, OR
12/07/2025